Hello, Gorgeous!

Tangled

BY TAYLOR MORRIS

GROSSET & DUNLAP
An Imprint of Penguin Group (USA) Inc.

GROSSET & DUNLAP
Published by the Penguin Group
Penguin Group (USA) Inc., 375 Hudson Street,
New York, New York 10014, USA
Penguin Group (Canada), 90 Eglinton Avenue East, Suite 700,
Toronto, Ontario M4P 2Y3, Canada
(a division of Pearson Penguin Canada Inc.)
Penguin Books Ltd., 80 Strand, London WC2R 0RL, England
Penguin Group Ireland, 25 St. Stephen's Green, Dublin 2, Ireland
(a division of Penguin Books Ltd.)
Penguin Group (Australia), 250 Camberwell Road, Camberwell, Victoria
3124, Australia (a division of Pearson Australia Group Pty. Ltd.)
Penguin Books India Pvt. Ltd., 11 Community Centre,
Panchsheel Park, New Delhi—110 017, India
Penguin Group (NZ), 67 Apollo Drive, Rosedale, Auckland 0632,
New Zealand (a division of Pearson New Zealand Ltd.)
Penguin Books (South Africa) (Pty.) Ltd., 24 Sturdee Avenue,
Rosebank, Johannesburg 2196, South Africa

Penguin Books Ltd., Registered Offices:
80 Strand, London WC2R 0RL, England

Text copyright © 2011 by Taylor Morris. Cover illustration copyright © 2011
by Anne Keenan Higgins. All rights reserved. Published by Grosset & Dunlap,
a division of Penguin Young Readers Group, 345 Hudson Street,
New York, New York 10014. GROSSET & DUNLAP is a trademark of
Penguin Group (USA) Inc. Printed in the U.S.A.

Library of Congress Cataloging-in-Publication Data is available.

ISBN 978-0-448-45528-0   10 9 8 7 6 5 4 3 2 1

To my niece, the fearless Sophie Rose—TM

CHAPTER 1

"Remember, Eve, you already promised me I could be your personal hairstylist," I said.

"Are you sure?" Eve asked. She sat next to me at the lunch table, a Frito pinched between her long, thin fingers. "Didn't I say umbrella holder?" She popped the chip in her mouth, then grinned.

"I'm not too proud to be an umbrella holder, whatever that is," Lizbeth said from across the table. "Just as long as I get to be there for your superstardom ride. And Kristen, too," she added, bumping her best friend's shoulder.

"I'll pass," Kristen replied.

"Well, *dahlings*," Eve said, tossing her long white-blond hair over her shoulder, "I'll see if I can fit you all into the payroll."

In case you were wondering, our friend Eve Benton was a huge star in our small Berkshires town. The biggest actress Rockford, Massachusetts, has ever seen.

After starring in a commercial for the live-action version of the video game Warpath of Alien Doom, Eve was still basking in the glow of the spotlight. The commercial's premiere and opening of the game a couple days ago had been a blast. There'd been a red carpet and lots of photographers taking pictures of the stars, and Eve had been the most glamorous of them all. At least in our eyes. She wasn't sure she wanted to be the next Disney star, but she was having fun with her newfound fame.

"Eve!" called Cara Fredericks as she passed by our table. "I saw the commercial this weekend. You were awesome!"

"Thanks!" Eve said, waving back.

"That was the best party I've ever been to," Lizbeth said. "I'd seriously go back to play the game if it meant I could walk that red carpet again."

"It was like sampling the life of a celebrity," I agreed.

"I liked having all of us hang out," Eve said. "That was better than the red carpet *and* the food."

"I'm pretty sure that there is no food in the world that is better than a boy," Kristen chimed in.

Eve had suggested we all bring dates to the premiere. My best friend, Jonah, went with her; his friend, Kyle, hung out with me; and Tobias Woods and Matthew Anderson, who Kristen and Lizbeth had crushes on, took them. Kristen, who liked to be in the spotlight, had paid more attention to Tobias than Eve. I knew that's why she was being extra snarky now. The attention wasn't on her.

"*Nothing* was better than the commercial," I said, bumping my shoulder against Eve's.

"Except maybe the hair and makeup," said Lizbeth, grinning.

Part of me cringed and part of me felt proud. Eve had played a blue alien goddess in the commercial, and that blue came out of a hair disaster created by yours truly. Thankfully, with the help of the pro stylists on the set, she had ended up looking amazing.

"Bunny wants me to go to Boston for more auditions, but Mom isn't so sure," Eve said. She picked the onions off of her ham-and-cheese sandwich. Bunny was the casting director who first spotted Eve when we were in the food court at the mall. "She wants me to agent up, even if I don't know if I want to commit to this acting thing."

"*Agent up?*" Kristen asked—with a bit of a sneer if I do say so. "What does that mean?"

"You know, get an agent," Eve replied. "Bunny said they'll set me up on auditions that I'm best suited for, stuff like that."

"That's so cool," Lizbeth said. "We've never had an actress at our school before."

"Or in our town," I added.

"You guys, it's no big deal," Eve said, blushing slightly.

"Yeah," Kristen said. "It's not like she invented leggings or something."

"Because then," Eve said, eyeing Kristen, "you'd all have to bow down at my feet. Right, Kristen?"

"That's not what I meant," Kristen said. We all looked at her and she withered under our gazes. "I'm sorry," she said quietly. "I wasn't trying to be snarky, okay?"

"You don't have to be my personal umbrella holder," Eve offered with a smile.

"Are you okay?" I asked Kristen. "What gives?"

"I don't want to be a downer," she said.

"Just snarky?" Lizbeth teased.

"You guys," she said, her voice close to a whine. Very unlike Kristen. "Look, Eve. I'm happy for you. I really am. I feel like a jerk." She sighed.

"But . . . ," Eve said.

"But . . . ," Kristen looked at Lizbeth and said, "You *know* how long I've wanted to be an actress. It's all I've ever talked about."

Lizbeth busted out laughing. "I've never once heard you say that."

"I say it all the time!" Kristen protested.

"Name one time," Lizbeth said.

"Look, the point is," Kristen said, ignoring her friend, "I'm really happy for you, Eve. And I also hope to one day be on TV, too."

"We can settle this right now." Eve looked around the table. "Whose phone has video on it? Can we get some live streaming here?"

"Very funny," Kristen said, but a smile crept across her face.

Lizbeth threw her arm around her and said, "We'll always love you, K. Even if you're a nobody."

Kristen nudged off her best friend. "You're messing up my couture blouse," she said. She ran her hands over the silk, pleated blouse she wore, smoothing out the nonexistent wrinkles.

"Don't worry, Kristen," I said, stifling a laugh. "No one will notice."

"Tobias might," she said. She looked around the cafeteria. "Where are they?"

"Seriously, Kristen," Eve said. "I'll give you Bunny's info if you want. You can call her and see if she can set you up."

Kristen picked at her food. "Maybe I will," she said, trying to be calm. But really, I knew she was bursting with excitement.

"That way you can see for yourself how boring a set

is," Eve continued.

"I would *love* to see for myself," Kristen said.

"And Kristen?" Eve said, really looking at her now. "All you had to do was ask."

"Fine, okay," she said. "I'm sorry, Eve."

"I know," Eve replied.

See why we're best friends? Even though Eve had only been at our school for a couple of months, she fit into the group like she'd been there forever. I don't know what I did before I met her. (Okay, I do—I hung out with my best guy friend, Jonah. But you know what I mean.)

After lunch, Eve walked with me to my locker to get my books for English.

"I'm already so behind on my reading," I said, pulling out the paperback copy of *To Kill a Mockingbird*. It had been assigned to us two weeks ago, but for the last week I'd been so focused on my oral presentation for our Career Exploration project that I'd let my reading slip. I'd given a presentation on my job as a sweeper at Mom's salon, Hello, Gorgeous! I really hadn't expected that to take up so much time since I've been at the salon my whole life. But now I was a couple chapters behind and I couldn't let Mom find out that I'd been slacking off or she'd make me step back from my responsibilities at the salon. "Want to come over after school to start studying for Friday's test? We can read the chapters together and go over them with those worksheets Ms. Carlisle gave us."

"Wow, Mickey." Eve grinned. "Start studying *now* for a test on Friday? Are you feeling all right?"

"Very funny."

Eve laughed. "I'd come over," she said, "but I'm busy today."

"Going to see your grandma or something?" I asked. That's the reason Eve and her mom moved here this spring—to be closer to her grandma. But Eve shook her head no. "Doing some mother-daughter thing with your mom?" She shook her head no again. "So come on," I prodded. "What are you doing after school?" This wasn't like her to be so secretive. I put on my best supportive friend face. I didn't want her to think she couldn't tell me something.

It was easy to see when Eve was embarrassed. She had really pale, smooth skin that flamed bright pink. "I have plans," she said slowly, "with Jonah."

"My Jonah?" I said. Then I gulped, realizing how that sounded. "I mean, my friend Jonah. Who is your friend now, too. I guess. Wow. Really?"

Eve gazed down the hall as she said, "We're just going to the Waffle Cone on Camden Way to get some ice cream before I meet Mom and Grandma for dinner." She was trying to play it cool, but I could tell she wanted to bust out a smile.

Eve and Jonah. Huh. When I first met Eve I wouldn't have paired them together, but now I saw that it all made sense. They had a lot in common, like video games and, well, me. I guess that was enough.

I wondered why Jonah hadn't told me about this. I knew they liked each other, but were they really considering dating? No way was Jonah ready for that. He still thought it was okay to burp in front of girls. I wondered why he wanted to stay close-lipped about my friend. Didn't I have a right to know what was going on?

(Okay, *maybe* not.)

We walked into Ms. Carlisle's English classroom and sat down at our desks, which were near each other.

"I wasn't planning on working at the salon today," I said. "But maybe I'll go in for an hour or two and then come meet you guys. What time are you going? Oh! Did you hear the Waffle Cone has a new tiramisu ice cream? Yum." If I went, I'd be doing Jonah a huge favor. Left alone, he'd probably think it was cool to show Eve his skateboarding scabs. Gross.

"Um, I'm not sure what time," Eve replied. She turned to get her notebook out of her bag, and then started flipping through her notes.

"You made plans but you don't know what time?"

I asked. I shook my head. "That's just like Jonah."

Eve didn't say anything. She just kept looking at her notes. That made me pause. "Wait," I said. "Are you guys together now or something? Like, *together* together?"

She blushed again. "I don't know," she said with a shrug. She still wouldn't look at me but this time I could see a real smile spread across her lips. "Friday at the premiere was awesome. We texted all weekend and then he called me last night. That's when he asked me out."

"You guys talked on the *phone*?" That was big. Bigger than talking at school.

She scribbled in her notebook. "Yeah. He said he couldn't wait until my next big premiere to do something so he asked me to hang out tonight. It was actually really cute."

It did sound sweet. Jonah wasn't just my oldest and bestest friend, he was also sort of like the brother I didn't have. But thinking about him being all mushy with Eve made a part of me grossed out. In a nice, happy-for-you kind of way, that is.

Ms. Carlisle finally got class started. She went over the chapters we read last week of *To Kill a Mockingbird* and as she talked about the trial and how significant it was that Jem, Scout, and Dill sat in the balcony of the courtroom, my mind drifted to my two best friends. How cool was it that they were dating! The three of us could hang out together, and maybe we'd all become best friends. It was win-win-win.

Before the last class of the day, I ran into Mr. Smooth himself, Jonah Goldman.

"Hey, Jonah," I called. "Wait up!" I ran down the hall to catch up with him.

He paused when he heard me, but didn't look up.

"Hang on a sec," he said. His eyes focused on the glow of his phone while he typed and sent a text. Once he finished he looked up. "What's up?"

"Hey, I was just wondering, do you know how long it takes us to walk to school in the morning?"

"No idea." He gave me a weird look. "Why?"

"Oh, I don't know, either," I said. "Not for sure, anyway, but I think it takes somewhere in the ballpark of eight minutes."

"Okay," he said. "So?"

"So . . . I'm just wondering why in eight solid minutes this morning you didn't tell me you and Eve have plans to go to the Waffle Cone this afternoon." I nudged his shoulder with mine and winked.

Jonah shrugged. "I don't know," he said, not meeting my eye. "Didn't think about it. It's not like it's a big deal or anything."

Aww, I thought I as I watched Jonah shift from one foot to the other. What a good friend! How sweet that Jonah didn't want me to feel left out. I'm so lucky to have two such amazing friends.

"I told Eve I might drop by to hang out with you guys," I said. "That's cool, right?"

For a moment Jonah didn't respond. Finally he said, "Yeah. Sure. I mean, whatever." He scratched the back of his neck and continued, "We're just hanging out. No big deal."

"Sure. No big deal. So you'll tell me when you guys are official, right?" I asked.

He cut his eyes at me and said, "Official what?"

"Her official BF," I replied.

"Biggest fart?" he asked.

Disgusting. But at least his immature joke made us both smile.

"You're such a dork," I said. "And be serious. If you guys get together then that's awesome. Right?"

"I guess," he said with a shrug. "Eve's cool."

"She's *cool*? Jonah, the weather in Canada is cool. My vintage barrette is cool." I touched said barrette—a long, crystal beauty I'd pinned on the side of my head that looked elegant in the midst of my barely tamed curls. "Can't you think of a better way to describe your girlfriend?" I said, testing the word on him.

"She's not my girlfriend," he said, just as I thought he would. He took his phone out again. A new text was on the screen.

"Okay," I said. "Sorry I said anything. But I just want you to know that she's my friend and you're my friend and if my two greatest friends are together—or just hanging out together or whatever you want to call it—then I think it's pretty awesome. Okay?"

He smiled the tiniest bit and said, "Okay."

We stopped at his classroom. Mine was just around the corner.

"Hey, you didn't tell me what time you'll be there tonight," I said.

"Maybe around four. But Mickey?"

"Yeah?"

He stood just outside the door and finally his eyes focused on me. He started to say something, but then seemed to lose his train of thought. "Never mind," he said.

I shook my head. Boys were always so distracted. "Text me," I said. "It'll be fun!"

CHAPTER 2

"Mickey, wait up!"

I turned to see Lizbeth and Kristen waving at me from the front steps just after school. I walked back toward them.

"Are you going to the salon?" Lizbeth asked. She shielded her eyes from the bright sun. "We're going for manis."

"Not today," I said. "I might go over to the Waffle Cone."

"Oh, come with us to the salon," she said.

I thought about Jonah, Eve, and the Waffle Cone. I didn't want to ditch them. Who knew what state of boy panic Jonah might get in if I wasn't there as a buffer. I also had a lot of homework to do. But the salon . . . it was my weakness.

"Yeah, sure," I said. "I won't get a manicure but I'll hang out with you guys for a little while." Chapter eighteen would still be there in a couple of hours.

We started the short walk over to Camden Way, the main street in town and where Hello, Gorgeous! was located. It was my mom's salon, and for my thirteenth birthday she finally let me achieve my lifelong dream of working there. I was the salon sweeper, but I also did whatever else anyone needed me to do. I kind of act as the stylists' assistant, getting them the supplies they need, helping to keep their stations clean, making sure the clients are comfortable and taken care of. Sometimes I even get to give my opinions on styles. It's basically the best job in the world. For now. Someday, I hope to run my own Hello, Gorgeous! and help Mom lead the style revolution.

As we walked down the tree-lined sidewalk, Kristen said, "Tell me it's not ridic that no one sells gold-and-silver sequined belts."

"Like a reversible belt?" Lizbeth asked.

"No, a mix of silver and gold in one belt," Kristen said. "Alternating."

"I don't know about the belts," I said, "but we have silver nail polish at the salon. Matte and metallic."

"What about gold?" Kristen asked.

"Just metallic," I said.

"We should invent a new color!" she exclaimed. "Matte gold with silver glitters. We'll make a ton of money. We'll be rich!" She did a little skip on the sidewalk in front of us.

"So are you going to make your fortune in polish or be the next Academy Award winner?" I asked.

"Does it matter?" she replied.

Fame. She didn't have it and already it had gone to her head.

"I thought all you ever talked about was acting," I teased, hoping it didn't make her mad.

"Very funny," she said.

"You were kind of on the attack at lunch today," Lizbeth said.

"I wasn't on the attack."

"But you *almost* were," Lizbeth said. "I could see it coming. Don't be jealous of Eve. She's our friend. It's not cool."

That's what still amazes me about best friends—you can tell the truth and the relationship just gets stronger.

"I'm not jealous," Kristen said with a little pout. "Eve deserves to be a big TV star. Getting all the attention."

"Jealous," Lizbeth said, shaking her head.

"Fine," Kristen admitted. "Maybe I was jealous for two seconds, but I'm over it because I'm going to make my own way in the biz. Didn't you just hear my million-dollar idea?"

"Yep," Lizbeth said. "Just want to make sure you're cool."

"I am," Kristen said as we headed up the last block

onto Camden Way. "Cool as a million bucks."

When we stepped through the doors of Hello, Gorgeous!, the sights and scents hit me like a warm, inviting hug. The cream marble floors, the chocolate-leather mirror frames, the honey-glow light, and all my favorite stylists making beautiful people even more beautiful. To me, there was no better place in the world.

"Hi, Mickey!" said Megan, the receptionist. She was always dressed to perfection—today she wore black leggings, a navy sweaterdress, and a chunky gold belt cinched around her waist. She greeted everyone who came through the doors with a smile stretching over her pink, round cheeks. "Are you working today? Hi, girls!" she said to Kristen and Lizbeth. They'd been coming to the salon for a while now getting manis and pedis and the occasional cut. We had all become friends after I started working here not too long ago. "Lizbeth, you're not back to take over my job again, are you?"

"I wish," Lizbeth said. She'd done her Career Exploration project at the salon, too, working the reception desk with Megan. "I'm temporarily retired from working."

Megan smiled. "I don't blame you. What are you girls in for today?"

"Manicures," I said. "Just for my friends."

"Sure," she said. "Go ahead and pick out your colors. I'll let Karen and Cynthia know you're here."

Kristen and Lizbeth hurried over to the wall of polishes.

"Is my mom here?" I asked Megan.

"She's back in her office."

"Okay. I'll go say hi in a bit." I walked over to my friends. I spotted a bottle of flat gray polish called Metal on Metal. "How about this?" I asked Kristen, handing it to her.

"I love it," she said, taking the polish.

"Or this one," I said, handing her a second choice. "It's shinier." Disco Ball was a lighter gray polish with tiny silver glitters in it.

"Ooh, I love them both," she said. "I'll take the shine." She handed back the first bottle and took Disco Ball over to the manicure station.

I helped Lizbeth pick out a color, too. She chose one called Strawberry Fields that was a deep pink, almost a red.

The girls settled in at the table. I pulled a chair up next to Lizbeth and sat against the wall. Karen raised her brow at me and said, "No manicure for you today?"

"Not today," I said. "I'll do my nails when I get home later."

"You think you can do them better than I can?"

Karen asked, her voice filled with mock concern.

"Of course not!" I said. "I just can't stay long today. That's all."

"Uh-huh," Karen said with a wink. But she knew I loved her designs. She often tested out the new colors on me each season.

I'd been coming to the salon with Mom forever, but it wasn't until I started working as a sweeper that I finally felt like I knew where I wanted to be. Getting to be around fabulous people and fun beauty products and styles made me feel like I was living inside my own personal fantasy world. I could talk about hair all day long and luckily, there was always someone who could talk it right back.

As Karen and Cynthia worked on my friends' nails, I settled back into my chair.

"Did you see Matthew in the halls after lunch?" Lizbeth asked. She had one hand soaking in warm, soapy water, while Karen filed the nails on her other hand.

"No," Kristen replied. She sat on the other side of Lizbeth. "What was he doing?"

Lizbeth gazed up and said, "Walking."

Kristen laughed. "Dork."

"He has the greatest walk," Lizbeth said. "Like, how he holds his books in one hand and keeps his other hand in his pocket. And he doesn't walk so much as *stroll*."

"Please," Kristen said. "Tobias moves through the halls with purpose. While your guy is taking his sweet time, mine is actually going places. Like to play baseball, where he is awesome. Matthew is too busy ironing his jeans."

"He doesn't iron his jeans," Lizbeth protested, and I laughed. "Mickey, he doesn't, does he?"

I pictured Matthew: super prep, always wearing button-downs or polos. Instead of sneakers he wore canvas shoes without a speck of dirt on them. "He might," I said.

"Ha-ha!" Kristen cheered. "He's a jeans-ironer!" When Kristen saw the pouty look on her best friend's face she said, "But it's cute, how nice he always looks."

"Especially Friday at Eve's premiere," Lizbeth said. "Oh my gosh, so cute. And he told me after we played the game that he'd have to bring me back sometime to practice more so that maybe I'd have a chance of winning." When Kristen and I didn't immediately respond she said, "He wants to go out again. With me!"

"Did I tell you that Tobias said the four of us should hang out sometime?" Kristen said. "He pretended to be casual about it but I knew he wanted to ask me out right then. So I was like, 'Yeah, we should go to the movies or something,' and he was like, 'Totally.' "

"Oh my gosh," Lizbeth said, bouncing in her seat. Karen gave her a look as she filed her nails, and Lizbeth settled down. "Do you think he really meant it? I had fun with Matthew and I think he had fun with me . . ."

As Lizbeth and Kristen dissected every moment of last Friday's premiere and all the tiny moments since, I wondered what exactly had happened to all my friends. I was starting to think they'd gone insane, like the aliens from Eve's commercial were taking over their minds. Except in this case, the aliens were boys. Boys we'd known forever, and who were just . . . well, boys.

I tried not to roll my eyes as Kristen explained how Tobias's little nod after lunch really meant *I'll text you later*, when the door to the salon opened and in breezed a woman you would never mistake for someone else. She had on-fire red hair in a long bob with perfect springy curls and wore a perfectly tailored suit. But most importantly, the glasses—black cat's-eyes with rhinestones in the corners. Behind the woman there was a man with a video camera filming Megan and the rest of the salon.

My jaw slowly dropped. I couldn't speak.

The woman walked up to Megan and asked to speak to the owner. She looked at a piece of paper in her hand. "Ms. Chloe Wilson?"

"Sure," Megan said, eyeing the camera nervously. She picked up the phone to call Mom in the back.

Kristen reached her freshly polished hand across Lizbeth toward me, her wide eyes on the woman. "Mickey. Oh my gosh, Mickey. Is that who I think it is?"

I felt my head nodding yes. The person I'd idolized since I learned the phrase "internationally acclaimed" was standing a mere six feet from me.

"It's her," I said. "Cecilia von Tressell."

CHAPTER 3

Lizbeth gasped. "Of *Cecilia's Best Tressed*?"

"Yes," I said, still not believing my eyes.

I stared at her as though I were invisible. Suddenly, her cat's-eye glasses were on me.

"Hello, girls," she said, strolling over to us.

"Hello," we said in stunned unison.

"Very pretty," she said, drawing an imaginary circle around my head. "The barrette—is it vintage?"

Oh my gosh, Cecilia von Tressell just complimented my barrette!

Cecilia is *everything* to the hair biz. She's worked all over the world styling hair for everyone from actresses to billionaires. She also has her own TV show, plus she runs a salon in Beverly Hills where she cuts and styles for the most exclusive clients in 90210. Next to my mom, she's one of my biggest idols.

"It is," I replied. "Thank you, Cecilia. I mean, Ms. Von Tressell."

She smiled. "You can call me Cecilia."

"It matches, see?" Kristen said, thrusting her hands out and practically knocking over her chair to get up. In one aggressive leap, Kristen stood in front of Cecilia. "They're both gray! Her rhinestone barrette and my polish. Right? They complement each other." She shook her fingers in Cecilia's face, then tossed a huge smile right at the camera. Then she winked.

Megan hung up the phone. "She's not answering. Mickey, will you go back and find your mom? She's probably in the break room checking inventory."

"Sure," I said. I stood on shaking legs and headed to the back of the salon, leaving Cecilia with Kristen.

"It's so funny you're here, *Cecilia*," I heard Kristen saying. "Because today I had the most amazing idea ever for a new polish. It's called Million Dollar Idea. It's matte gold with silver glitters and maybe there could be a signature accessory and hairstyle that go along with it. What do you think? No one has ever done that before."

I found Mom in the break room. My heart raced with excitement as I said, "Mom. Brace yourself."

"Hey there, sweetie," she said, looking over her shoulder while counting shampoo bottles. "When did you get here?"

I loved how crisp she still looked even though she'd been at work for more than seven hours. Mom never looked anything but perfectly put together.

"Not long ago," I said. "Mom, listen. Something is happening."

She turned back to the shelf. "Good or bad?" she asked.

"*Very* good. There's someone here to see you."

"Tell them I'll be right out," she said. She made a few notes on her clipboard.

"Well, it's actually . . ." I felt like a scream of excitement was about to soar out of my mouth. "It's Cecilia von Tressell!"

Mom continued to inspect the shelves. "How do I know that name?" she asked.

Are you kidding me? I wanted to yell. I couldn't believe it. *How does she know that name? Is my mother a hair goddess or not?*

"Mom," I said. She finished what she was writing, then looked at me. "Cecilia von Tressell is the host of a TV show called *Cecilia's Best Tressed*. She goes to salons all across the country, analyzes them, and makes them even better. She takes salons into the big time."

"Oh, of course. I remember hearing about her. She's supposed to be extremely talented," Mom said. "What's she doing here?"

29

That's when a slow realization washed over me. The moments from more than two months ago ran through my mind like an old home movie. Me, watching *Best Tressed*. A commercial, with the announcer asking viewers to text in their recommendations for the next salon makeover. Me, texting in.

And now, they were here. Mom's salon was going to be famous because of *moi*!

"Well," I began slowly, drawing out the suspense. "A couple of months ago, I texted in that Hello, Gorgeous! should be featured on the show. And now they're here! Can you believe it?" I wanted to jump and clap but somehow managed to maintain my cool. This was Mom's moment.

Mom stopped what she was doing. She straightened up and turned to face me. "What do you mean, *they're here*?"

"Cecilia's here. With her show!"

"With her show?"

"And cameras!"

Mom set her clipboard down. She put one fist on her hip and stared at the table. I knew Mom wasn't the type to go all giddy. I guess she needed a moment to collect herself. It *was* momentous.

"You're telling me," she began, "that you invited a camera crew into my salon for some reality show without my permission? Without *anyone's* permission?"

"No," I said. "It's not like that. I mean, yes, I just texted the show to enter the salon. But it's not a reality show, really. It's more like a . . . like a showcase! About the best salons in the country!"

"If my salon is so great, why is she here to *make it over*, Mickey?" Mom asked, eyeing me fiercely.

"Mom," I said, trying not to panic. I didn't think she'd be upset. "She just observes the salon for a couple of days, makes some recommendations, *gives you free money* to make some changes, and then they show all the work you've done!" I thought surely the free money part would get her excited.

"And that's it?" she asked. "I'm expected to believe that's the entire show? No drama over how I make any possible changes? I just do it and she comes back and says it's great?"

"Well," I began, "it's a little more involved . . ."

"Oh, Mickey."

"It's okay, Mom!" I said. "The only thing is after her final inspection she sort of, like, deems your salon a revamped success. Like, maybe it's still good but not great."

"Not great?" she asked, her eyes about popping out of her head.

Oops! "It's just the lingo," I said, trying to calm her down. But no dice.

"Mikaela Wilson, do you understand the position

you've put me in?"

My face burned under Mom's glaring eyes. "Mom, it's okay," I tried again. "Cecilia's very nice. She's going to help you!"

"Who said I needed any help?" she said. She sighed, rubbing her temples. "Well, I have no choice now. They're here, filming. I can't not go out there. I can't say *no* on camera."

"Well, I mean, you can," I said. "People have done it. But, Mom, I really think this could be amazing. Think of the great exposure you'll get. And I know you won't let anything go wrong."

"*You* better hope nothing goes wrong, Mikaela," she said. My skin went cold. Mom doesn't call me Mikaela when I've done something right.

She brushed her still-perfect, thick black hair off her face, smoothed her still-crisp slacks, and walked out to the main floor.

CHAPTER 4

As soon as Mom's heels hit the floor, the staff erupted into applause. Everyone knew that *Best Tressed* was a huge opportunity for any salon or stylist. Giancarlo clutched Violet's arm, practically bouncing in his black-and-white oxfords. Devon, across the salon, had her arms crossed like she wasn't so sure about the whole thing, but I could see a curious sparkle in her eyes. Piper wiped away happy tears as she clapped, and even Karen looked blown away as she discreetly straightened her station in between her own claps of approval.

Kristen still stood next to Cecilia, talking to her as she clapped. When Mom approached Cecilia, reaching out to shake her hand, Cecilia carefully nudged Kristen aside to make room for Mom. Then Cecilia spotted me and motioned for me to come join them.

The camera swooped over me and Mom, its light shining in my eyes. Mom had a smile on her face, but I knew it wasn't real. Did I ever mention that she likes surprises about as much as uncombed hair?

Cecilia stepped between me and Mom. It was probably best for everyone if there was a buffer between us right now. That plastered-on smile of Mom's was pretty scary.

"As I understand it," Cecilia began, "it was you, Mickey, who recommended Hello, Gorgeous! to my show. Is that correct?"

"Yes," I said.

"You wrote, and I quote"—she held up a small black notepad and read—"'Hello, Gorgeous!, my mom's salon, is the best place to make any person feel gorgeous. My mom works hard each day to make sure that every single person who comes into her salon feels like herself when she leaves, only better. Mom's salon is the greatest and deserves to be made even greater.'"

I'd forgotten what I'd written. I peered around Cecilia at Mom to see her reaction. But she kept that fake smile plastered on and I knew that inside, she was boiling.

"Now, Chloe," Cecilia said, a mischievous smile on her face. "Your salon is good, but we think it can be great. Do you want to be known as fine or do you want to be known as fabulous? This isn't Cecilia's Okay Tressed, or Good Tressed. It's *Cecilia's Best Tressed*. We'll work with you to give you all the tools to take your salon up a notch. But it will take your own fire, passion, and creativity to make your salon an even greater success. So, Chloe Wilson, I have to ask you—are you ready to be Best Tressed?"

Mom turned to Cecilia, her fake smile stretching even wider. "Absolutely," she said. "At Hello, Gorgeous!, we settle for nothing less than the best."

The stylists burst into applause again.

"Great!" Cecilia called out over the cheers.

Cecilia gave Mom and her staff a quick rundown: For the next three days, she would personally inspect the salon to get an idea of how the place worked and what services Mom offered. On Friday, the stylists would be observed by Cecilia's expert team, the Head Honchos, to get a deeper understanding of how the stylists worked their craft. At the end of the day, Cecilia would make her recommendations on how to make the salon even better. Mom would have until Saturday evening to make the changes. Then Cecilia would review the work on Saturday night and decide if Hello, Gorgeous! could join the ranks of the Best Tressed.

"Now, Miss Mickey," Cecilia said to me. "Since this was your idea, I'd love to have you here each day, showing me the ropes and such. If the boss agrees, that is." She peered over her glasses at Mom.

"We'll see if it fits in with her schoolwork," Mom said. "We'll see."

"That's good enough for me," Cecilia said with a wide smile.

Everyone buzzed with excitement as Cecilia told Mom that work would begin first thing the next morning. Then the cameras shut off. Mom and Cecilia went back to Mom's office to talk more business.

"Mickey, I can't believe it!" Lizbeth said, rushing up to me. "Your mom must be blown away!"

"I'm shaking," I said. I still couldn't believe this was happening. "I can't believe she's here. And we're going to be on her show!"

"We are!" Kristen exclaimed. "Do you think she liked my idea of pairing a nail polish with a hairstyle? I made it up on the fly when I saw her, but it might be something really cool. Don't you think?"

"I guess," I said. I was still trying to process everything that was happening. Hello, Gorgeous! was going to be famous. Mom may have been nervous walking into this (see: Mom and surprises), but I knew she would soon realize how great this was going to be.

CHAPTER 5

The front door slamming. That's how Dad and I knew Mom was home. It's also how I knew things were not going to go well.

We heard Mom drop her bag on the living room floor with a slap and kick off her heels with a crumple.

"Mickey!"

I looked at Dad.

"Don't worry," he said as he patted my shoulder. "She's in here," he called out.

When I got home from the salon, I'd told Dad everything. The texting, the camera, the fake smile. He seemed to agree that Mom was in a momentary panic but would come around to see how great this could be for her and the salon. "But just in case," he'd said, "we better have a great dinner waiting for her." We'd gone to Antonio's, a fancy Italian place she loved, and brought home the works.

Mom padded into the kitchen in bare feet, her tailored pants dragging on the floor now that her three-inch heels were off. Her hair had some flyaways and her blouse was slightly untucked. She rarely looked disheveled, even at home. The woman didn't even own a pair of sweatpants. This was bad.

She pursed her lips and stared me down. "Mikaela," she began. "Honestly."

"Now, Chloe, hang on a second," Dad said. "Before you get upset, let's talk about this."

She looked at him with way too much confidence. It was a little freaky. "Upset? Who said I'm upset? I think it's just great that my thirteen-year-old daughter is making monumental business decisions for me. Who wouldn't want—"

"Chloe," Dad said. "Settle down. Please."

Mom narrowed her eyes at Dad. Then she looked at me, crossed her arms, and said, "Explain."

I gulped.

"Mickey told me about the show when she got home, and it sounds like it'll be great for your business," Dad said, stepping in. "She said it's the highest-rated show on the Perspective Network."

"It's still a *reality show*," Mom said. "The whole point is to embarrass the people silly enough to agree to go on!"

"Mom," I said, "this is, like, the most respected

show on TV about the salon industry. Have you ever seen a single episode?"

"I know *of* Cecilia von Tressell. But, no, I've never seen her show."

"Well, come on. I'll show you an episode. We can eat while we watch. Dad got Antonio's."

"Antonio's, huh?" She looked at Dad. "Sounds like you two are really trying to work me over."

"Come on," I said, pulling her by the wrist into the living room. "You'll see!"

We set up a fancy Italian picnic on the living room floor and watched one of my favorite episodes. It was set in Chicago at a salon attached to a swanky hotel. When the cameras showed the salon at the beginning of the episode, you couldn't imagine how it could get any better. But with Cecilia's keen eye to the fabulous, by the end of the episode it looked like the kind of salon that even the biggest-haired pop star might be intimidated to go into (but still would, of course).

"See?" I said once the show had ended and we'd gobbled up all the eggplant lasagna and garlic bread. "It's a great show! She doesn't make you look bad. She makes you look even more incredible."

"I have to say, Chloe," Dad said, "I think Mickey's right. I don't think you have anything to worry about."

"You don't?" Mom asked, still wary.

"Not at all," I said. "It's not like Cecilia's out to get you. She's one of the best stylists in the world. I heard she did Princess Catherine's hair for her wedding." I wasn't exactly sure about that, but I'm sure Cecilia could do an amazing princess look without it being too princessy.

"See?" Dad said to Mom. "If the Princess of England trusts her, then you've got nothing to worry about!"

Mom leaned against Dad. "I don't like the idea of being scrutinized, especially not on TV. But maybe . . . maybe it'll be good exposure?"

"Yes!" I said. "I knew you'd get excited about it!"

Mom eyed me. "Do I look excited?"

I didn't respond—but *no*, in case you're wondering, she did not look excited.

"Look," she said. "I appreciate what you were trying to do, and I understand that you probably didn't really think we'd be picked. But we were and I don't like being surprised like this. However, I do agree that it could be good for business. As for what Cecilia said about you being there every day . . ."

"Yes?" I asked, hopefully. All I really wanted out of life was to be at the salon every second of every day.

"If you can get all your schoolwork done well and on time, then I think it'd be fine for you to come in each day this week. You could help me from making a fool out of myself."

I couldn't believe it. I was going to be on TV with Cecilia von Tressell. I was going to get to know her! Work with her! Learn from her!

"I will totally be there every second of every day that you let me," I said.

"Good," Mom said with a smile. "Now let's clear out these dishes and start up another *Best Tressed*."

This was amazing. I had to call Eve and tell her everything, especially since she was the only one who didn't know yet.

After clearing the dishes, Mom and Dad settled in for another episode. I grabbed my phone and ran back to my room.

When I opened my phone to call Eve, I realized I had five texts from Kristen.

Do you think I'll need to sign a waiver for being on camera today? Because I totally will.

Should I make an appt for Sat? That's when the final reveal is, right?

If I make an appt do u think I'll 4sure be on camera, or maybe?

Should I call Eve's agent, Bunny, and tell her that I've already been on camera? Or does that hurt my chances?

Wait, do you think my scenes today will end up being cut?

Sheesh. I guess Kristen had found her way to be famous. I sent her a quick text back:

No idea about most of your questions but make an appt, anyway. It's going to be fab! TTYT.

Then I called Eve. When she answered, I heard explosions, laughter, and yelling before finally, "Hello!"

"Eve?"

"Hello?"

"Eve, it's Mickey," I said. "Can you hear me?"

"Mickey? Speak up, I can't hear you!"

"Where are you?" I asked.

"Warpath Live Action," she said. Then she said something I couldn't understand because of all the noise.

"You're at Warpath?" I asked. "What are you doing there?" Her voice kept cutting in and out thanks to bad reception. But I did hear the name *Jonah*. "Eve, listen, I have exciting news. You won't believe what happened. Hello?"

". . . can barely hear you."

"I have really big news!" I practically shouted into the phone. "You won't believe it!"

"Mickey?" she said as another round of explosions blasted in the background. "I can't hear you. I'll call you back, okay?"

"Okay," I said. "Call me back!"

We hung up, and I sat back on my bed holding my phone. I'd completely forgotten about hanging out with her and Jonah at the Waffle Cone today. I hoped she wasn't mad that I never showed.

I wondered what she was doing at Warpath. She was supposed to be at dinner with her mom and grandmother. But it was dinnertime now and Warpath was at the other end of Camden Way, and it sounded like Jonah was with her now.

"Mickey," Dad said, poking his head in my room. "Come on down. We're going out for dessert."

I looked at my phone and realized I'd been sitting there for an hour waiting for Eve to call me back. But I guess she forgot.

CHAPTER 6

"You know what it is?" Mom said the next morning at breakfast. "After watching a couple of episodes of *Best Tressed* last night, I realized that it's not only good for business, it might even be fun."

"That's the right attitude," Dad said. "You'll have the kind of exposure that never would have been possible."

Mom sat at the table in her long silk robe and gently blew on her tea. "I just have to remember that Cecilia is making a television show, and I am receiving invaluable business advice. I have to make sure I keep all the drama out. It'll be Cecilia's most boring show yet."

"Mom, how can you say that?" I said, setting down the bacon, egg, and cheese on an English muffin Dad had made. "You've never wanted to do anything poorly."

"My goal isn't to do a poor job. But some of those owners and staff get very dramatic, fighting over what changes are going to be made or doing a tacky job of renovating," she said. "I won't have any of that. Everyone will be as professional as they are every day, and whatever renovations or changes Cecilia suggests we make are going to be perfect."

I picked a piece of bacon out of the sandwich. "It's going to be amazing no matter what. Didn't you see how glamorous Cecilia made all those salons? When she's done with you," I said, popping the bacon in my mouth, "you'll be fit for Newbury Street." That was like the Rodeo Drive of Boston.

"Mickey, if I want to be fit for Boston, I can do it on my own," she said. And it was just like Mom to say that. She didn't want anyone else's help because she didn't *need* anyone else's help. Or so she thought most of the time.

"Shouldn't you be heading out to school?" Dad asked me as he finished the last of his breakfast sandwich.

"Where's Jonah?" Mom asked. She looked out our back doors toward his house, which was directly behind ours. "He never misses breakfast."

It's true. He came over most mornings to scarf down our food like we were the local diner and he had an open tab.

"Not sure," I said, gulping down the last of my

orange juice. "I'll see you at the salon this afternoon."

Knowing I'd be on camera today—and every day this week—I'd dressed carefully this morning. Not too flashy, but professional and stylish in a white dress with thick green, yellow, and red diagonal stripes.

I was walking to school alone wondering why Jonah hadn't come over, when guess who I spotted walking up the front steps to school? Eve and Jonah. I hurried to catch up with them, and that's when I noticed that Eve was wearing Jonah's Red Sox hat. His *favorite* Red Sox hat. She looked really cute in it, her white-blond hair swept into a low side ponytail. They walked inside together, and I followed slowly. Something about the hat and the walking together made me not want to barge in on them. I stopped in the hall to untie and retie my shoe. I dug around in my backpack, looked through my phone, and straightened my dress. Then I went to try to catch Jonah at his locker.

When I got there, Jonah was alone, digging through the mess of books and folders. I nudged him in the shoulder. "Hey."

"What's up, Mickey?" he said, glancing over at me.

"You on a diet or something?"

He furrowed his brows. "What do you mean?"

"You hardly ever miss breakfast at our house. Or

our walk to school."

He shut his locker and we started down the hall to mine. "Sorry. I came in early."

"How come?"

"Just wanted to get some extra studying in."

That made sense, I guess. I thought of the chapters I'd tried to read last night for English. *Maybe I should come in early and study, too.* "Well," I said, "you're missing all the action. You won't believe what's happening at the salon."

"Uh-oh," Jonah said, looking at me with a slight smile. "What now?"

"It's nothing bad!" I said. "It's amazing. You know that show I always watch called *Cecilia's Best Tressed*?"

"The one I always run away from when it comes on your TV?"

"The one you secretly like," I teased him. "Yes. They're here in town to do a show on Mom's salon!"

"Whoa," he said. "Seriously? That's amazing."

"I know, right? And it's all because of me. I texted in to enter Hello, Gorgeous! I never thought they'd actually show up. Or at least, I thought they'd give us some warning."

"Nice job, Mickey," he said. We were at my locker, and I did a quick change of books and folders. "How's your mom holding up?" He knew exactly how intense she could be.

"Pretty well." I decided to keep my copy of *To Kill a Mockingbird*, just in case I found some extra time to read before class. "Just utterly determined for everything to go perfectly."

Jonah smiled. "Of course she is. I bet it's going to be great, though."

"I think so, too."

As we parted ways to go to our classes, he said, "Just let me know if you want me to come in and make a scene."

"Don't you even."

"Oh, yeah, I forgot," he smiled. "That's your department."

"That is so not funny," I called after him.

After multiple boring classes, Eve caught up with me on my way to lunch.

"Hey, Micks," she said, practically skipping up beside me. "Want to go to my locker with me real fast, get my lunch?"

"Sure. Hey, sorry I didn't show up at the Waffle Cone yesterday. I guess you survived without me." She smiled. I looked at her hat and said, "Or maybe barely. What's with the hat?"

Eve tugged on her side ponytail and said, "I was just having a bad hair day."

"I think your hair would look adorable if you took

off the hat. Is that Jonah's?"

"Actually," she said as we got to her locker and she spun the combo, "I have to wear it because of a bet I lost." She dumped her books, grabbed her lunch, and we headed toward the cafeteria.

"What bet?" I asked.

A big, silly grin spread across her face. "Okay. So. Last night we were having ice cream right after school, right? And Jonah dared me to take this big bite of my ice cream. Like a huge chunk, teeth and all." I cringed thinking about freezing ice cream on my teeth. "If I did it, he said, then he had to buy me a game at Warpath. If I didn't then I'd buy him a game. I have really sensitive teeth but I had to take the bet. Couldn't do it, though." She laughed. "It was so cold on my teeth and I opened my mouth and, like, ice cream oozed out onto the table. Very graceful."

"Classic," I muttered.

"So then—okay, wait," she said, trying to remember the events. "First, we met my mom and grandmother and they invited him to dinner, so he came along. Then I asked Mom if we could go to Warpath after dinner and she said fine. We were only there for an hour, though."

"How'd you get," I said, pointing to my head, "the hat? Again, I mean."

"Oh!" she said. "It was another bet. I really thought

I could beat him at the game but he slammed me. Twice. So I have to wear his hat all day today, except in classes, of course."

We were almost to the cafeteria and I didn't want to be all moody during lunch, so I asked, "So that's why you didn't call me back last night?"

"Oh my gosh," Eve said, putting her hand to the bill of the hat. We sat at our table, where Kristen and Lizbeth already were. "That's right—you said you had news. I'm so sorry, Mickey! What is it?"

Kristen looked up from her turkey-and-avocado sandwich and said, "You haven't told her yet?"

"I haven't had a chance," I said, getting all excited again.

"Tell me! Tell me!" Eve said.

"Have you ever seen that show *Cecilia's Best Tressed*?" I asked.

"Only every single episode of every single season."

"Well . . . guess who came into Hello, Gorgeous! yesterday?" I asked.

Kristen and Lizbeth sat on the edges of their seats, waiting for Eve to guess everything.

When Eve realized what was happening, she said, "No way. I don't believe you. For real?"

All three of us nodded.

"I am totally and completely serious," I said. Then I told her how I texted in to the show, not thinking anything of it until Cecilia showed up yesterday.

"Hello, Gorgeous! is going to be on *Cecilia's Best Tressed* and they start filming today!"

"So that's why you look extra cute," Lizbeth said, eyeing my dress.

"Thanks," I said. "And check this out: Since I was the one who texted the show, Cecilia asked if I could be there each day this week to sort of help show her around or whatever. And Mom agreed. She said I got her into this mess so I had to suffer with her."

"Suffer? That is awesome," Kristen said, shaking her head. "I wish she'd ask me to come in, too. If you need any extra help—"

"I'll let you know," I laughed.

Jonah and Kyle came over with their lunches and sat down at our table. Jonah sat next to Eve, and Kyle sat across from Jonah, an empty seat between him and Lizbeth.

Eve swatted Jonah's arm and said, "I can't believe you kept such big news from me last night."

"I just found out about it today!" he said.

"Last night?" Kristen asked, a mischievous look on her face.

Eve blushed and said, "Um, we went to play Warpath."

"*And* get ice cream," I teased. I almost added the dinner part, but Eve was turning so red that I decided to back off. She was smiling, though.

"Hey," Lizbeth said. "Why are you wearing that hat?"

"Don't ask," I said, stopping her before she could answer. I caught eyes with Kyle, and he shook his head and sort of rolled his eyes like, *Ugh. Those two.* I gave him a look back that I hoped said, *For real.*

"Whatever," Kristen said. She was a master at bringing one conversation to a halt and changing it to another direction—usually toward her. "Can we please talk about how I'm going to make my debut?"

See?

"Yes," I said. I tapped the table. "Everyone, we're talking about Kristen now."

"When do we not talk about Kristen?" Kyle said, and we both smiled at our jokes.

"Ha-ha, not funny," Kristen said. "Mickey, I made an appointment for Saturday. What do you think?"

"We don't know what time they'll be shooting the finale yet," I said.

"Well, I figured there's also Be Gorgeous, and they'll definitely film that, right?"

"Probably."

"You know she can't actually guarantee you'll be on the show, right, K?" Lizbeth said.

"Of course," Kristen said, like *duh.* "But as soon as word spreads that Hello, Gorgeous! is going to be on *Best Tressed*, appointments are going to fill up. I have to do what I can to help myself. There's enough room in this town for two TV stars."

"Hey," Eve said, but to Jonah—not us. "I found out about that skydiving thing we were talking about last night. I was watching *MythBusters* . . ."

Eve and Jonah stayed in their own conversation for the rest of lunch while Kristen, Lizbeth, and I talked about what Cecilia might really be like, and if she would be mean or nice (depending on the salon, she could be pretty firm). I had to admit Kyle was kind of on his own with Jonah being so into Eve. I felt bad, but then got distracted when Kristen and Lizbeth said I had to make sure I upped the glam before going to work after school.

"How dare you!" Gesturing to my outfit, I said, "The glam *has* been upped!"

"I mean your makeup," Kristen said. "The camera doesn't show much makeup, so you have to put extra on just to look normal."

"Is that true, Eve?" I asked. She was the only one of us who'd seen herself on camera.

"What about that part when they collided in midair?" Eve asked Jonah.

"Hello, Eve," I said, shaking her shoulder. "Are you listening?"

"Sorry, what, Mickey?"

"So, Jonah," Kyle said very pointedly. "I never told you about that new skating trick we've been trying."

Jonah turned his attention to Kyle and Eve finally turned back to us.

"We were wondering," I said, shooting Kyle a grateful look, "if you have to wear extra makeup on camera for it to show up. Did they put extra on you for your commercial?"

She shrugged. "I don't know about regular makeup, since I was wearing silver and white, but they did put on a ton."

As we headed out of the cafeteria after lunch, the girls continued talking about how I should look for my first day on camera. My stomach started to get a little tight. I was excited to get to the salon but I was starting to get a little nervous, too. Being on camera wasn't exactly routine stuff.

After waving good-bye to the girls and Jonah and Kyle, Eve and I walked to English together.

"I hope I don't say or do anything dumb on camera," I told Eve. "That'd be just like me."

"You won't!" she said. "You'll be totally fine."

"Should I remind you that you're talking to the person who creates disasters and crises on a weekly basis?"

Eve smiled. "I think you're going to be great. Just do what you do best—help out at the salon."

Before I could get to the salon, though, I had to get through English class. Ms. Carlisle was cruising through *TKAM*, and it turned out I was actually two full chapters behind. I was supposed to have read through chapter twenty-four—which meant that the chapters I'd read last night (and barely concentrated on) weren't enough. I knew I should be taking notes as Ms. Carlisle gave her lecture, but I couldn't stop worrying about what would happen at the salon—that afternoon and for the rest of the week. I had to make sure everything went smoothly. I wanted to show Mom how great this whole Cecilia thing could be for her and Hello, Gorgeous!

CHAPTER 7

Every time I walk through the doors of Hello, Gorgeous! there's a certain buzz in the air. Something's always happening. People are gossiping, getting and giving advice, being pampered, made over, and beautified. But today, with Cecilia and her camera crew hovering around, there was no buzz—more of a contained hum.

Cameramen were all over the salon—I did a quick count of four. Cecilia walked slowly across the floor, her arms folded over her toffee-colored jacket. She stopped to inspect a cut Violet was finishing up. Violet stepped back as Cecilia looked at the woman's chin-length hair, showing new angles to Violet and talking to the client. It wasn't until Violet laughed with Cecilia that I realized things were going just fine.

"Mickey, hi," Megan said. "Are you here to help us out?"

"Yep! All week," I told her, leaning slightly on the reception desk to really take in the scene before I jumped in myself.

A camera was all up in Devon's station as she combed out her client's wet hair. She looked a little annoyed but I also noticed she looked extra cute today. Devon always sported a rockabilly look but today she had cranked it up. Her black bangs had just been trimmed, and the black dress with red accents she wore hugged her body perfectly. Looking around, it seemed that everyone was a little more stylish than usual, which was amazing because everyone always looked great. Even the chunky necklace and bracelets Megan wore seemed more sparkly than normal.

"How's Mom doing?" I asked Megan.

"She's, um, fine," she said. "You know how your mom is!"

Yes, I totally knew how she was. But Megan would never say anything negative about my mom.

"I better go get ready," I said. I went toward the break room in the back, which doubled as a storage area. I took the heinous plastic smock Mom forced me to wear as the sweeper out of my cubby, put it over my shoulders, and snapped it on. I couldn't believe I'd be on camera for four days in this thing. I mean, really—it's hard to have dignity when you're working in a shower curtain.

On my way to the front, Mom came barreling out of her office and we totally collided.

"Goodness! Mickey!" she said, sucking in her breath and looking about as relaxed as a germophobe picking through the trash. "Did you sweep my station? I have a client due here any minute."

Before I could answer, she hurried away toward the front as a camera caught sight of her and followed. I didn't want to make her any more nervous, so I quickly grabbed the broom and went up to check. Mom was straightening up her always-perfect station, and there wasn't a single hair on the floor. I ran my broom around it, anyway, knowing it would help calm her down.

"Violet, your technique is wonderful, really," Cecilia was saying. Violet's station was right next to Mom's, so I could hear it all. "How long have you worked here?"

"Going on seven years now," Violet said. Her ultrashort, golden-blond hair was perfectly styled, not moving a bit as she combed and cut her client's dark hair. "I've been manager for two."

"Well, you certainly have talent," Cecilia said. She looked at Violet's client in the mirror. "This cut is going to look gorgeous on you. Absolutely stunning."

The client smiled and said, "I'd never go anywhere else."

"Thank you, Mickey," Mom said, interrupting my eavesdropping as I swept microscopic dust off her station. She practically shooed me away. Her client was coming, and Cecilia turned her attention to Mom. I backed away, getting more nervous at what was about to happen. Would Cecilia be extra hard on Mom just because she was the owner? Would that make good TV? I almost couldn't watch. (But of course, I did.)

"Hey, kid." Giancarlo's voice boomed down at me from the other side of Violet's station. He nodded his bald head for me to come closer. A camera was behind his shoulder, catching his every cut, but he looked relaxed and comfortable.

"Hey, Giancarlo," I said, feeling a bit jittery with the camera so close and so *on* me.

"Mickey, could you do me a huge favor? Could you please tell Miss Lisa here how gorgeous she's going to look with these long layers I'm about to give her?"

I felt myself blush under the scrutiny of the camera. I looked at the woman in his chair as she smiled at me expectantly. She had a freckled face and dark green eyes. I wondered if Giancarlo was just playing it up for the cameras. "Most definitely," I told Lisa. "Giancarlo is the master of long layers."

"And I didn't even have to pay her to say that!" Giancarlo said.

"Not this time, anyway," I said, and Giancarlo

winked a *thanks* at me.

I glanced back at Mom. Cecilia was observing her as Mom consulted with the woman in her chair. Mom now looked relaxed. Maybe because she was totally in her element and knew everything was perfect as long as she stood behind the chair with comb and scissors in hand.

The salon continued to work in overdrive as cameras caught our every move. Cecilia strolled past the stylists, inspecting each and every cut, color, and blowout. She didn't say too much, but having someone watch over your shoulder can be a little tough. I even felt her eyes on me as I ran to get a drink for Giancarlo's client. It frazzled me enough that I grabbed the wrong drink twice. First I got a diet and then I brought back a seltzer.

"Mickey, did you leave your head back there?" Giancarlo teased. "She just wants a Coke, sweetie, that's all."

After I delivered the drink, Cecilia approached me. "Your mom has a fantastic salon here," she said, looking at me through her kitty-cat glasses. "Did she know you texted her in for the show?"

"No, it was a total surprise," I said, then added, "but a good one." Of course, a camera was right between us, making sure to get every word that came out of our mouths.

"Do you want to go into the business as well?" Cecilia asked.

I tried to ignore the big black camera and shining light above it and just concentrate on this one subject I loved more than anything. "Definitely. I want to be just like my mom. I want to cut here when I get older and then maybe open my own salon one day."

Cecilia nodded. "Do they help you with your own hair? It looks very healthy—a nice, glossy shine."

"Devon did," I said. "She showed me how to tame my curls."

"It's a good lesson to learn," she said, pointing to her own spiral, red curls. "Do you think you could get my guys here something to drink? They've been hiding behind these cameras for a while."

"Thanks, Cee," said the voice behind the lens.

"Yeah, sure," I said.

I got sodas for the guys and then I showed Cecilia where we kept the cotton robes the clients wore and where we stored extra products. By the end of the day I felt totally comfortable around her, just like I did with the other stylists. Suddenly I didn't care that she was on TV—or, I guess, that I was, too.

As her crew packed up she thanked my mom for a great first day.

"And Mickey," she said, turning to me before leaving, "thank you so much for all your help today.

I look forward to tomorrow."

Mom looked at me and gave me a nod of encouragement. "You're welcome, Ms. von Tressell. And me too," I said.

"Remember, you can call me Cecilia," she replied. "See you all tomorrow!"

When the door closed and the crew was gone, everyone in the salon let out a sigh of relief.

"We made it," Giancarlo said, collapsing against the back of his chair.

"Great job, everyone," Mom said. She really seemed to mean it, too. First day down, four to go, and everything looked great in Gorgeousland.

At home Dad was finishing up a special celebration dinner for our first day with Cecilia. While he put on the finishing touches, I ran upstairs to call Eve and tell her how awesome the day went.

"I knew it would be great," Eve said.

"*So* great," I said. "I was nervous at first, especially being on camera, but after a while I sort of forgot about it."

"Reality people are always saying you get used to it," Eve said.

"I know, right? And do you know what I was thinking?" I could hear her typing through the phone.

"Wouldn't it be awesome if your commercial came on during my show?"

She didn't respond. I heard the fast tapping of keys and then a giggle. "Eve?" I said.

"Oh, sorry! What'd you say?"

"If your commercial came on during our episode of *Best Tressed*—wouldn't that be awesome?"

"I know," she said. "I mean, yeah, it'd be awesome."

"I can't have a huge premiere party like your commercial did, but we should definitely have some party here at the house for it, don't you think?"

"Uh-huh," she said, clackity-clacking on her end.

"Eve!" I said. "What are you doing?"

"I'm listening!" she said. "I swear."

"So what'd I just say?"

"You said they're going to make a commercial of the show you're on."

"Not even close," I said. "And tell Jonah I said hi."

"Sorry, Mickey. Don't be mad. He was just IMing me a question about our English homework."

"I'm not mad," I said. And I really wasn't. I was in too good of a mood to be upset. Dad called up from the kitchen to say dinner was ready. "I gotta jet, anyway. I'll tell you all about it tomorrow, though. Kay?"

"Definitely," she said.

As I headed back downstairs, I heard Mom telling Dad about the day.

". . . amazing job," she was saying.

"You didn't expect any less, did you?" Dad asked. There was no reply, and Dad said, "Oh, Chloe. She's excellent at the salon."

I stopped short just outside the dining room.

"But she has had a few problems in the past," Mom said. "You can't deny that. Today, she was incredible, though. Mickey really took it upon herself to help Cecilia out. I didn't even have to ask her. She was more calm than I was with those cameras on her. Seeing her so in control made me feel relaxed, too. She doesn't even know how much she helped me."

I helped Mom? That seemed totally impossible. My mom was always poised and perfect and in control. How could a spaz like me keep her calm?

"Maybe you should tell her," Dad said.

I took that as my cue to walk into the dining room then, as if I hadn't been listening. Dad had set up a total feast for dinner—braised short ribs with homemade fries and bread with some kind of fancy cheese. I even spotted what looked like my favorite dessert— raspberry cheesecake—on the counter in the kitchen.

"Wow, Dad," I said as I sat down. I tore off a piece of bread and spread the cheese on it. I took a bite— creamy and buttery and delicious. Through a mouthful I said, "This looks amazing."

"I had to do something special for my girls on their

first big day in front of the cameras," he said. "Mom was just telling me that it went pretty well."

Mom sat down and Dad served up the short ribs.

"Mickey, I wanted to tell you," Mom began. "Last night I really wasn't feeling a hundred percent about this whole TV thing. But after today, seeing how Cecilia worked with my stylists and hearing her initial thoughts, I feel very good about it." She piled fries on her own plate and sprinkled sea salt on them from the dish in the center of the table. "I was just telling Dad how proud I am of how you handled yourself today. You did a great job."

"That's our Mick!" Dad said, always ready to cheer me on.

"I had a lot of fun," I told them. "Cecilia is really nice."

Mom nodded. "She has a lot of great ideas, just after the first day. This could turn out to be huge for the salon. She mentioned expanding Rowan's spa area. I know it's really small, but I just haven't put the time into thinking about what to do with it. She's also looking at Karen's manicure station and seeing how we can expand that, too. Really turn the place into a full-service salon."

"That all sounds great," Dad said.

"It is," Mom said. She looked at me and said, "All thanks to this one."

I gobbled up my dinner, as happy as I'd been since I started working at the salon. I'd finally done something Mom was really impressed by.

After dinner, I knew I should be reading *To Kill a Mockingbird*, but I couldn't help going online for just a couple of minutes to see what else I could learn about Cecilia. Soon, I was weaving through links and going from site to site, learning all these really cool things about her. Like how she was raised in the Midwest but always wanted to live in New York City, so as soon as she graduated from high school she moved there all on her own. I read about her first job at a salon in the city (as a sweeper!), and how she rose through the ranks to become the youngest stylist in the salon's history. I read for so long that I almost forgot I was supposed to be reading something else—a certain classic for English class. Oops.

CHAPTER 8

"You should have seen her hair," I said to Eve at lunch the next day. "Like electric red, but not harsh. And I think it's natural. Well, mostly."

"That's so cool," Eve replied.

"Yeah, except I totally didn't read anything for English. Did you?"

"Yeah, the book is really good," she said. "Hey, give that back." She turned to Jonah, who had just swiped a chip from her lunch.

"I'm an animal!" Jonah said. "A wild beast who takes what you're not fast enough to eat!" Then he reached over and grabbed another chip from the pile.

"Jonah!" Eve laughed. "You have your own lunch."

"I'm a growing boy!"

"Boy is right," I muttered. But at least I got a

laugh out of it. From Kyle. "Seriously. What is with these two?" I asked him, jerking my thumb toward them.

"I think they've been infected," Kyle said.

I grinned. "Aliens? Body snatchers?"

"Stupidity," Kyle said. I agreed.

"Eve," I said. "Are you going to come to the salon while Cecilia is there? Maybe we can get you on camera."

"No, you said he was the best gamer of all time. Which totally isn't true," Eve said.

If what Eve just said to me made no sense, there's a good reason for that. It's because she wasn't talking to me. She was talking to Jonah. Still.

I shook my head and turned back to Kyle. "I think we're both right. They've been infected by stupid alien body snatchers."

"That's exactly what I've been saying for a week!" he said.

"And by the way, where are Kristen and Lizbeth?" Lunch was almost over but they still hadn't come to our table.

"I'll give you a hint," Kyle said. "Argyle socks."

"Oh no," I said, immediately understanding. I looked over to the next table and sure enough, Kristen and Lizbeth were sitting with Tobias and Matthew. Tobias might not be the type to wear preppy socks, but Matthew totally was. Matthew was saying something and the girls—especially Lizbeth—looked totally captivated. "Should we call the nurse?"

"Unfortunately, I think they're a lost cause. No antidote strong enough. It's too bad, really," Kyle said, gazing off at the other table as if in deep thought. "I was just starting to get slightly less annoyed with them."

"The girls or the guys?" I asked, picking up my bottled water and taking a drink.

"Both, of course," he said. "I mean, Tobias is the greatest player in the history of baseball. Didn't you get that memo?"

"Jonah, let go!" Eve said, laughing and leaning away from Jonah—and onto to me—as he tugged on her wrist. She jerked her hand back, which banged into my arm. The one holding the bottle. Water spilled down the front of my shirt.

"Ugh, real nice," I said, looking down at the wet spot. Eve didn't even notice. She and Jonah just kept goofing around.

"It's safe over here," Kyle said, nodding to the empty seat next to him and across from me and the mutants.

"Thanks," I said, pushing my tray across the table, then walking around. I dabbed my napkin on my shirt, trying to dry it. "Don't worry! I'll be fine!" I said loudly to Eve, but she barely glanced my way. "I think we should pick up some masks from the nurse," I said to Kyle. "You know, so we don't breathe in their disease." I looked back at Tobias and Matthew and pretended to be seriously observing them. "Okay, Tobias is obviously the king of baseball."

"Obviously. And Matthew is the duke of argyle."

"So that means Kristen is . . . ," Kyle began.

"Be careful," I said. "Those are my friends."

We both watched them. Kristen was trying to spoon-feed Tobias some of her chili, but he brushed her hand away. Then he reached over and snatched the bite from her, anyway.

"Kristen is the princess of persuasion. And Lizbeth is her lady-in-waiting," Kyle said.

"Well done, sir," I said. "So what does that make us?"

"Court jesters, of course," Kyle said.

"Perfection."

As we dug back into our lunches, I thought about how boy-crazy all my friends had become. Kristen and Lizbeth had been crushing on Tobias and Matthew for weeks and weeks and they were just now finally talking to them. Well, maybe *talking* wasn't the right word—more like giggling hysterically. Didn't they know that guys are normal people (mostly) and they didn't have to act like that around them? They're actually really easy to talk to. You just sit down and . . . talk. Presto!

"It's a battle out there," I said to Kyle. "We can't let them take us."

"You're right," Kyle said, matching my serious tone. "We have to stick together or our brains will melt."

"Melt into stupid alien body snatchers soup."

"I think that's what they're serving at lunch tomorrow," he said, turning to look at me with a small smile. I smiled back and took a bite of my sandwich.

We watched as Jonah challenged Eve to thumb wrestle—which she refused—then Eve challenged Jonah to rock-paper-scissors instead. I shifted in my seat just as Eve bopped her "rock" on Jonah's head, wondering if I should make another joke to Kyle or ask something about him.

Kyle cleared his throat and said, "Hey, so get this: Jonah and I had plans to take our bikes to the top of that trail above Camden Way. You know that one I'm talking about?"

"Yeah," I said. "Bended Brook."

He turned his head slightly to look at me. "Yeah. Have you ever done it?"

"No," I said. "But I've always wanted to. I heard you can see the whole town from the top."

"Right. So Mr. Love over there made plans to go with me tomorrow after school. We were going to ride up to the top on our mountain bikes. But guess who's bailing?"

"No way," I said. "Jonah canceled on you?"

"Yup," Kyle said. Jonah and Eve were so wrapped up in whether paper covered rock that we didn't even have to lower our voices to talk about them. "Supposedly they're going to study together."

"Oh, gag," I said.

"I'm still going," Kyle said. "You can come with me if you want."

"I don't have a mountain bike," I said, wishing more than anything that I had a mountain bike. I had no idea Kyle did such cool things.

"That's okay. I mean, we can walk the trail," he said.

I really wanted to go—it sounded amazing. But I'd have to ask Mom if I could be away from the salon for one afternoon, since Cecilia wanted me to be there. I felt lame telling Kyle I had to ask for permission so I said, "Yeah, okay, then. That'd be cool." And I hoped it would be.

"Awesome," he said.

Kyle and I spent the rest of lunch talking to each other since everyone else had gone crazy and abandoned us. It was like we were the only two sane people left.

CHAPTER 9

When I got to the salon after school, Cecilia was at Devon's station, watching closely as Devon cut a woman's chin-length black hair, while a camera captured it all. Two other cameras roamed the salon but everyone seemed much more chill about it today.

"Hey, hon," Mom said from reception when I came in. "Cecilia was asking about you."

"Really?" I asked, excited.

"She wanted to make sure you were coming in today," Mom said. "You must have made an impression on her."

This made me feel amazing, totally incredible. So while I was feeling fab and Mom was, too, I figured it'd be a good time to ask her about tomorrow and hiking with Kyle.

"Hey, so, um," I began in my signature smooth style. "Do you think it'd be okay if I went hiking with a friend after school tomorrow? I'll come here first to see if you need anything. If that's okay?"

"Are you going with Eve?" Mom asked as she thumbed through receipts.

"No," I said. "My friend Kyle."

She paused and raised an eyebrow. "Kyle?"

"He's a friend of Jonah's, too."

"Ah," she said, setting down the receipts and giving me her full attention. "Jonah's going as well?"

"No," I said. "Just me and Kyle."

Mom nodded slowly, considering this. It made me feel like I needed to explain myself more. "Eve's spending a lot of time with Jonah lately and now Kristen and Lizbeth are hanging out with these boys they've liked for decades," I said. "So that leaves me and Kyle, fending for ourselves. We thought we might as well hang out together."

Mom brushed my hair off my shoulder. "Is everything okay with your friends?" she asked.

"Of course," I replied, giving a little shrug.

"What about your homework?"

"I have a test on Friday but I'm caught up on my reading," I said. *Mostly*, anyway. Except for not reading those chapters last night. I could totally catch up, though.

"All right," Mom said. "Come by the salon first tomorrow, just to check in. And I want to see what chapters you've read before you go to bed tonight. If it's done, then you can go."

"Thanks, Mom," I said. I was already thinking about what I should wear tomorrow. Did I have a good hiking outfit?

"You sure everything's okay with your friends?" she asked again, a worried expression on her face.

"Yes," I said. "They're just busy with boys." I didn't tell her I was getting a little annoyed with the whole thing. It was frustrating that I couldn't have an uninterrupted conversation with Eve, or that Kristen and Lizbeth had entirely ditched our lunch table to sit with Tobias and Matthew.

I didn't want to admit I was a little worried that I was starting to lose my friends.

Mom rubbed my back and said, "If you're sure you're okay. But I want you to start on your reading as soon as we get home."

"Consider it done," I said.

I went to the back to put away my stuff and put on my smock. I realized I was pretty excited about tomorrow. Hanging out with Kyle would be like hanging out with Jonah, and I hadn't done that in forever.

And knowing that Cecilia was impressed with my help yesterday really made me want to step it up today. I wanted to show her that I was not only helpful at sweeping up and bringing supplies, but also amazingly good at hair stuff. I could be like her someday, and she could help get me there.

"Hi, Cecilia!" I said when I came out from the back, snapping on my smock. She was inspecting the hair-washing sinks, the chairs, towels, and products we used. She wrote everything down in her black notepad. Her black skirt suit fit her perfectly, the jacket flaring out over her hips. She even had rhinestones on the lapel, tying the look into her signature glasses.

"Hello, Miss Mickey," she said. "Good to see you again."

"Can I get you or your crew anything?"

"No, I think we're all set," she said. She picked up one of the towels and ran her hand across the fabric.

For a rare moment there was no camera over her shoulder. I thought it was the perfect time to try to learn more about her. The articles I'd read last night were great, but I wanted to hear some of Cecilia's stories from the woman herself. "So, um, I read online that your very first client was your mom," I said.

She smiled. "I was fourteen when I first cut my mother's hair. It was a disaster. Totally lopsided in the back, bangs butchered. And I had used dull scissors, which damaged her ends even more than they probably were." She laughed at the memory.

"I colored my friend's hair blue," I admitted,

thinking what a bonding moment this could be for us.

Her eyes widened. "Is she still your friend?"

"Miraculously, yes," I said with a laugh.

"Lucky you," she said, looking relieved. "Did she keep the blue?"

"Only for a day. But she looked amazing, especially when I added the makeup," I said. It had felt incredible to create a look for Eve's commercial, even if it came out of my mess-up. "She was shooting a commercial when I colored her hair," I told Cecilia. "I did her makeup to tie the whole look together since we couldn't fix her hair right away. The makeup artists on set liked it so much they used it for her and all the other actors."

"That sounds very impressive," Cecilia said.

"Yes! I mean, thanks. Have you seen it yet? The commercial? If you want to see what I did maybe we can look online—"

"Mickey!" Violet called from her station. She motioned to the floor.

"Don't let me keep you," Cecilia said. "Just pretend like we're not here."

"Okay, sure." But come on—how could I step away when I had Cecilia von Tressell all to myself? "How old were you when you got your first job in a salon?" I asked.

"I was nineteen, so you have a head start on me,

that's for sure," she said. "Now, better get back out there."

I didn't want to look like I was slacking, so I took my broom back to the floor and got to work sweeping Violet's station. "Sorry about the wait," I told her.

"No worries. You looking for fame on film or something?" she asked, nodding to one of the many cameramen wandering around the salon, including one that was back on Cecilia.

"No, not fame," I said, because that made it sound cheap. I wanted to be respected. I wanted to be successful. "I was just making sure Cecilia didn't need anything."

I started to sweep, but Mom came over and asked, "Do you want to help me with this client? We're doing a complicated updo. I just need someone to hand me bobby pins as I twist and sculpt her hair."

"Sure," I said, excited for the task. Watching my mom work was even better than actually working. She was a master and made it look so easy.

The rest of the night went well, customers coming and going a bit more than usual. Kristen had been right—word had definitely gotten around town about what was happening at Hello, Gorgeous! and people wanted to try to get on camera. Of course, the salon gave priority to its loyal clients, asking walk-ins to wait—but always with a smile and a soda from Megan.

I didn't want to bother Cecilia with questions again, but I did send friendly vibes her way throughout the evening. They finally paid off while I was stocking fresh towels by the sinks.

"Excuse me, Mickey?" Cecilia asked.

"Yes?" I said eagerly.

"Do you have a moment to show me something?"

"Of course!" I said, because *hello*!

"Great," she said. "Your mom is busy with a client and I'd like to take a look at the supply closet, see what kinds of products you keep on hand and how much."

"Sure, of course," I said, putting the rest of the towels on the shelf above the sink. "Right this way!"

She followed me to the back, and even though she'd been roaming the salon for hours, I wanted to make sure she—and future viewers—knew where everything was and that we were well prepared.

"These are the changing rooms for the clients," I said, showing her the door to the dressing rooms. "The robes—well, I already told you about them, but they're very luxurious." I grabbed one off the hook and said, "See? Feel." I wanted the viewers to know that Hello, Gorgeous! went the extra mile to make clients feel comfortable, and this was just one tiny bit of evidence.

"Yes, I see," Cecilia said. I'm sure she had a whole

closet full of cotton batiste robes and shirts, so she knew the quality of it.

"We also take care in washing them on the gentle cycle," I said, leading her to the back.

As we passed the door to the basement Cecilia said, "What's behind that door?"

"Don't even think about opening that door," I said quickly, "unless you want to be dinner for the zombie rats. They have a whole colony down there. We tried to evict them but they won the battle, so." I shrugged. "What are you gonna do?"

The whole time I was thinking, *Ha-ha-ha, look how witty I am!*

"I'm sorry," Cecilia said, pausing beside the door. "Zombie rats?"

I nodded. "Crazy, huh? Anyway, back here is where we keep the products since we can't keep them down there."

"Mickey, darling," Cecilia said.

Darling? She must really be feeling me! Like I'm her long-lost daughter or her business partner!

"Did you say rats?" she asked.

"*Zombie* rats," I clarified.

Cecilia eyed me with a slightly horrified expression. I guess zombie rats can do that to a person. And then I saw it. The red light just behind Cecilia's shoulder. Camera lens aiming right at me. My stomach dropped, realizing that I had just been recorded on camera for all of the world to see.

"Did you get that?" Cecilia said, turning to the camera guy behind her.

I wanted to leap out and grab the camera. Destroy the tape, erase all the evidence. Would they leave that in the final edit for the show? They knew I was joking, right?

Cecilia started to move on, but I reached out to stop her. I stammered, "I mean, totally teasing about that. Mom sent an exterminator down there. It's all cleaned up! The bugs, I mean. And rats. Actually, I'm not *exactly* sure there were ever any rats. I mean, that would be gross, right? It's just like, really messy down there. That's all." I was starting to sweat, thinking of how Mom would react if she knew what I'd said.

"You sure about that?" Cecilia peered at me over her cat's-eye glasses, scrutinizing me like an X-ray. I'd never felt so exposed.

"Yes! I mean, we used to have a tiny bug problem but the exterminator took care of it. But no rats. Ever!"

"What's the basement used for?" Cecilia asked. "Storage or something?"

"Um, yeah, we use it for storage," I said. "Now, right back here is where we store those products you were asking about." I tried to lead her away from the basement door but she still stood beside it, looking curious.

"You don't store the products in the *storage* basement?" she asked.

"Um." This was not happening. I would not say stupid things to Cecilia von Tressell on camera that made my mom look bad.

"Could you please show us the basement?" Cecilia asked.

"Uh, I can't," I said.

Cecilia raised an eyebrow and said, "Why not? Is it that unsafe down there?"

"Not at all! It's safe as a baby's room!" I moved my body ever so slightly in front of the door. "It's just that Mom has the key, and I know she left it at home, so maybe some other time." Like when the cameras were long gone. "Now, the products you wanted to see are right back here."

I showed her the products in the back, and she made a special note that the space doubled as the staff break room. I tried to tell her all sorts of interesting things about the salon in a pathetic effort to make her forget about the zombie rats, but even if I wasn't smart enough to keep my mouth shut, I was smart enough to know she'd never fall for it.

CHAPTER 10

That night, after spilling my mother's deep, dark basement secret to a future nationwide audience, I locked myself in my room and concentrated on reading chapter twenty-eight of *To Kill a Mockingbird* and preparing for Friday's test. I got totally caught up in the chapters and completed the study worksheets Ms. Carlisle had given us. After inspecting my work Mom said, "I'm proud of you for working so hard—at the salon and in school. You deserve a day off." Which just about killed me since I may have made her and the salon look like a major health-code violator. I went to bed feeling anxious about what the show would do with all that rambling footage of me.

Cutting-room floor, anyone?

In the morning, I felt less anxious about my latest salon goof. It would all be okay, I told myself. No one would care about a dirty old storage basement with all that styling going on upstairs. I decided to focus on my afternoon with Kyle.

I had a hard time coming up with an appropriate outfit—one that would take me from school to salon to wooded trails. After spending more time digging through my closet than I'm willing to admit, I finally came up with something appropriate: slim khaki pants with an army-green-and-tan layered tank with a jacket over it.

Kyle planned to meet me near the front office after school. I spotted him waiting for me, leaning against the wall as he looked down at his cell phone.

I went up to him and playfully punched him on the shoulder. "Hey."

His face relaxed into a big smile, showing off that front tooth that very slightly overlapped the other, just enough to be charming. "You ready?"

"Yep," I said. "Do you mind if we stop by the salon so I can check in with my mom, make sure she doesn't need anything? We can leave our bags there, too, if you want."

"Yeah, sure," he said as we headed out of school. "And maybe we can go to the Waffle Cone afterward to grab some ice cream or something before heading home."

"Sure," I said. "I still haven't tried their new tiramisu flavor yet."

We walked over to Camden Way to drop off our bags. "Be warned," I said before going into the salon. "There are cameras."

"Oh, right," he said, as I opened the door. "That TV show. You gotta tell me all about it."

"I'll tell you after," I said. I had Kyle wait at the front while I quickly walked to the back to stash our stuff.

Mom was in her office. "Hey, Mom," I said, peeking through the doorway. "I'm here—okay if I go?"

She smiled. "Everything's fine here. Go have fun with your friend."

I dashed back to the front and . . . uh-oh. Giancarlo was hovering over Kyle. The poor kid looked like he was being interrogated by the Secret Service. But even worse, a cameraman had spotted them and was on his way up to capture it all. I raced ahead of him.

"Hey, GC," I said. "Bye, GC!" I grabbed Kyle by the wrist and pulled him out the door. We ran halfway down the street before slowing down.

"Who was that guy?" Kyle asked, catching his breath.

"Just Giancarlo," I said. "What was he saying to you?"

"First he asked if I had an appointment. Then he asked if I needed some product for my hair. And *then* he asked what my intentions with you were."

"Oh my gosh," I said, completely mortified. "What did you say?"

"I said I was going to show you the town." He shrugged. "I panicked."

That was actually really sweet. I mean, I know what he meant—that he was showing me the view of the town from the top of Bended Brook. But it sounded cute.

"Giancarlo is harmless," I assured him. "He's like my uncle at the salon."

"What's going on there, anyway? I know you guys were talking about it the other day at lunch, but what's the full deal?"

"I got my mom on a TV show." I sounded like a show-off, I know, but who cares—it was just Kyle. We turned off the main road and onto a small wooded trail, barely wide enough for us to walk side by side. Our arms brushed against each other.

"Wow," he said, stepping in front of me to hold back a thin branch that was hanging over the trail. I stepped around it before he let it snap behind us. "I didn't know you knew people in the industry."

"Ha-ha," I said. "I'm exaggerating. A little. But I did text the show and tell them Hello, Gorgeous! should be featured. I didn't think they'd actually do it, though."

"So what happens?" he asked. "Is it, like, a competition or something?"

"No, it's more of a showcase," I replied. I wasn't sure that was the exact word but it definitely wasn't a competition. I told him how Cecilia picks a salon to observe for a week, sees how things run, and how the vibe is. "Tomorrow, her Head Honchos will come in to observe the stylists on their techniques to get a deeper understanding of the salon. And then Cecilia will make her recommendations on what to change to take it from good to great, and Mom has about twenty-four hours to do it."

"What if your mom doesn't make the changes?" Kyle asked. "Watch that rock."

I stepped around a jagged rock sticking up from the ground and said, "Lots of times on the show the owners freak out and get really upset about having people tell them what's wrong with their business. Sometimes they refuse to make changes. But that's not going to happen with my mom. She has the most successful salon with the best stylists in New England for a reason. She doesn't freak out. Mom is always in control—especially at her salon."

"That's cool," he said. The sun streamed through the vibrant green leaves of the trees, casting a bright light over us. "I can't believe there's another thing being filmed here. First a commercial and now a whole

TV show. Rockford is becoming the Hollywood of the Northeast."

"We can rename it Hollyrockfordwood," I said.

"Martin Scorsese will want to shoot his next gangster film here," Kyle joked.

"And you'll get the lead role of the godfather's ruthless son, ready to take over the family business."

"Yeah," he said. "I'm the only one in town who hasn't been on camera yet, now that you've got that Cecilia chick here. Your friends must be going out of their minds to get on TV."

"Not really," I said. Then I thought of Kristen. "Well, one of them. I think Lizbeth would like to be on as well but she's not making a big deal of it. Eve, though, couldn't care less."

"But isn't she supposed to be the actress?"

"I don't think she cares about it that much. Especially since she and Jonah got *together*." I said the word as if it were a big whoop-dee-doo.

"Those two," Kyle said. "They've seriously lost it."

"I know. I really think we should investigate this alien theory because they are not acting normal."

"I was actually thinking about calling the authorities," Kyle said. "The body-snatcher police."

"But how will we know the body-snatcher police are the *real* police? What if they've been body snatched, too?"

"Because," Kyle reasoned. "If they've been snatched they won't hear a word we say."

"That's true," I said. I thought of how lately, when I tried to talk to Eve, it was like she wasn't listening. To anyone but Jonah, anyway. "Maybe we can try to rescue them. Save them from themselves. Because seriously—how lame have they been acting?"

"Dude, if Jonah doesn't pull it together soon I'm going to have to give him a serious beat down on Warpath of Doom."

"What I don't get is how they can just ignore their friends. What's that about? I mean, here we are in the woods fending for ourselves."

"Like we've been thrown to the wolves."

"Yes, like wolves," I said.

"No, we're thrown to the wolves," he said.

"That's what I said."

"No, you didn't," he laughed.

"Don't laugh at me," I said, lightly punching his arm.

Kyle dodged my hand and leaned back. He howled a huge laugh before doubling over and actually slapping his knee.

"Hilarious, Kyle," I said. And then I started laughing, too, because he had started laughing for real.

The trail to the top ended in a short, steep climb and we had to use our hands to help pull ourselves up.

"The top is right up here," Kyle called back to me. "This is a good foothold right here."

I put my foot in the spot he showed me and pulled myself up. The climb was tough but I didn't want to look like a wimp so I worked every muscle to hoist myself up. I dug my hands and nails into crevices in the rocks for support, glad I hadn't gotten a full manicure.

When we got to the top, the rock was wide and smooth. We walked to the edge and looked down at the town laid out before us.

"Wow," I remarked. "Pretty nice."

"Yeah. Not bad."

We stood for a moment as the sun started to dip, casting a soft glow over our town. A white church steeple peeked up from the tops of the trees on the horizon and the cars on the winding streets below looked like toys from up on our perch.

After a while Kyle said, "We should get back before it starts getting dark."

"Okay," I agreed. I knew he was right, but I kind of didn't want to leave. The view was so cool. I wished I could show Eve and the rest of my friends. *Eve would totally like doing this*, I thought. *Lizbeth, maybe; Kristen, no way.*

We started down the trail, careful of our footing on the climb down.

"I can't believe Jonah would bail on this," I said. "He loves outdoor adventures, and it's amazing up here."

"I know, and imagine riding mountain bikes down this." He kicked a rock, sending it rolling down the trail ahead of us. "I'm thinking we need to help our friends. We have to show them they're missing stuff like this."

"Totally," I said. "I mean, a study date? It's like, what next? Checkers on Saturday night?"

"They're becoming old people like our parents."

"More like our grandparents," I said. "We have to show them that the whole world isn't just the two of them."

"We should actually do that."

"Maybe I should remind Eve of all the fun stuff she likes to do with her friends," I said, thinking. "I'll get her to go out with me and the girls tomorrow night. If I can get them away from Tobias and Matthew."

"Let's stick with one operation at a time," Kyle joked.

"Agreed. Okay." I starting to think this could be a real plan. "I'll make sure Eve and I hang out tomorrow night. You're in charge of taking Jonah out."

"I'll take him skateboarding after school and maybe we'll go play video games at the mall," Kyle suggested.

"Perfect. We just have to make sure they agree to

go out with us and not each other. Can you handle that?"

We got to the end of the trail and started back on the sidewalk. "I can handle it," he said. "So do you want to go to the Waffle—" His phone chimed just then and he checked the new text message. "Oh, brother. It's my mom." He shut off the screen and said, "Dinner." He rolled his eyes. "I guess ice cream another time, then."

"Yeah, no problem," I replied. I'd had a great day hanging out with Kyle. Boys could be really cool, and you didn't have to go all mental over them.

We headed toward Hello, Gorgeous! to get our bags. The cameras were gone and I was glad to not have to face them. I raced to the back and I brought our bags out to where Kyle waited on the sidewalk.

"Thanks," I said as I handed over his bag. "I had fun. Eve and Jonah have no idea what they're missing."

"So we're on? For our plan?"

"We're on," I said.

Kyle stuck out his hand. "Deal?"

I took his hand in mine.

"Deal," I said.

"We'll get that ice cream some other time." He let go of my hand and started down Camden Way toward his house.

As I watched him go, butterflies soared in my stomach and all I could think was, *What was that?* That strange feeling of nervousness I got when Kyle held my hand. That's totally not something that should happen between friends. Is it?

CHAPTER 11

Later, at home, I started reading the last three chapters of *To Kill a Mockingbird* for the test tomorrow.

My mind kept drifting to Eve and what fun things we could do tomorrow night, though. It had to be something amazing to drag her away from Jonah. Maybe Kyle and I could brainstorm, help each other come up with ideas. After all, he knew about Bended Brook and that was something I'd never have thought of on my own.

I started thinking about Kyle and how there were never any awkward pauses in conversation and how sweet he was helping me up the trail even though I didn't need it. I thought about the branch that stuck out in the middle of the trail that he held back, and how he made sure I had good footing on the climb to the top.

I wondered what that little zip was that had gone through me when we shook on our plan.

Is that what happens when you like a boy? That feeling that makes you go all giggly and crazy like Kristen and Lizbeth? If so, count me out. Kyle and I could act normal around each other.

I shook off those funny feelings and focused on the mission we had agreed on. I had to remind Eve that it was actually really fun to hang out with her girlfriends. Girls had to stick together; isn't that what we were taught? Maybe for starters I could invite her to the salon for a full beauty treatment. I didn't think she'd mind being there while the cameras were shooting.

Then I started to wonder what was going to happen to Hello, Gorgeous!, how it would be different just after being on the show. Tomorrow Cecilia would make her recommendations, and I could hardly wait to hear what she had to say.

I put my book down and sat at my vanity table. It had a three-way mirror so I could see all angles of my hair. I played with some styles while I waited for dinner and planned out my Friday night with Eve. When I heard the front door shut, I figured Mom was home. I went downstairs.

Dad stood at the island in the middle of

the kitchen cutting up vegetables for a salad. Mom paced back and forth, a tight expression on her face.

"Hey," I said. "What's for dinner?"

Mom turned on me and sucked in a deep breath. "Zombie rats?" she practically hissed.

Oh no.

"Wait, that's not right," Mom continued, putting her finger to her chin as if she were thinking very hard. "*Mutant* zombie rats. Did I get it right? Is that the correct wording, Mickey?"

Dad stayed quiet, which meant I was in deep trouble.

"Mikaela," Mom said. She threw her hands up. "I just . . ." She shook her head, then looked to Dad. "What am I going to do?"

Dad put down the knife and walked over to her. Mom sat down in a chair and rested her elbows on the table, cradling her head in her hands. I'd never seen her so upset to the point of speechlessness before. It scared me.

"Come on, honey," Dad said, giving her a hug. "You're overreacting."

"No," she said. "It's not even everything that happened at the salon, or everything that Cecilia said." Mom looked at me through weary eyes. "It's that having the cameras there to capture it all is too much pressure. It's not just some fleeting moment of embarrassment for me or the salon. It's recorded to be played back *forever*."

I thought of all the times I'd messed up at the salon—and there were a lot. How would I feel if all my mistakes had been caught on camera for the world to see again and again? It was bad enough for my mom and my friends to see me mess up. I didn't know if I could take it if there were a constant reminder of that sitting in someone's DVD collection.

Dad sat next to Mom and said, "Tell me what happened."

"She caught me off guard," Mom said. "Which was probably the point. They have to make a good TV show, right? Cecilia and I were talking about how long Rowan has been doing facials. Cecilia commented that the room she works in is pretty small—which it is, I know it is. And then she said, 'Maybe you can kick out the mutant zombie rats and make better use of that basement.' I didn't know what she was saying at first, but then she asked me if I was really allowing an infestation of rats to live in the basement. An infestation! That's what she said. Mickey, you know I've had an exterminator down there—there are no bugs, and certainly no rats. It's just messy, that's all. But I didn't want to show Cecilia because then she'd think I'm disorganized and not on top of things."

"I told her all that," I piped up. "I said you had an exterminator and that there weren't any rats down there. I didn't show her anything, though!"

Dad rubbed Mom's back and said, "Chloe, I'm sure it's not that bad."

"Mom, it's a makeover!" I said, trying to get her to see that this could be a good thing. "The basement is like a hopeless case of dry, frizzy hair with bad coloring that *only you* can transform into something beautiful. You just have to step up to the chair and work it!"

"She's right," Dad said. He gave me an encouraging smile.

Mom looked at me. "I trusted that this reality show stuff would be something good and fun for my business. But, Mickey, this doesn't feel very fun right now. Not to mention that tomorrow is the day Cecilia makes her big recommendations. Who knows what she'll say."

"Mom, I'm sorry," I said, my stomach tightening at the mention of tomorrow's big day. I'd never seen her so defeated. I started to think maybe this was a bad idea after all, but I didn't want her to give up yet. *I* didn't want to give up yet. *Cecilia's Best Tressed* was about making a salon the best it could be. I wanted the whole world to know that Mom's was the greatest salon, even if we did have a messy basement. "Did you show her the basement?"

"I had to," Mom said. "I'm contractually obligated to go along with this nonsense. And I'm sure this is exactly the kind of TV she's looking for. She has to up the drama somehow."

I could only imagine how Cecilia reacted. There may not have been any bugs, but it was pretty messy down there. Aside from the metal staircase and dangling bulb on a chain, the basement was full of boxes overflowing with old products that never sold, broken and burned-out hair dryers and flat irons, grimy towels that were never washed or thrown away, and a rusty sink that only sort of worked. It may have been a bug- and rat-free zone, but it was still a mess—definitely not something Mom would want her clients or potential clients to see.

"I agreed to do this show because I honestly started to think that you were right," Mom said wearily, looking to Dad. "I thought that it could bring in more business, really take Hello, Gorgeous! to the next level. But I meant the next level up, not down. I don't know how to fix this."

"Mom," I started.

But she stood up from the kitchen table and looked down at me. "Where's your homework—have you done it yet?"

"Not yet," I admitted.

"I shouldn't have to be the one to remind you

that you have a test tomorrow. I expect you to be responsible, Mickey."

And I knew she meant more than just the test. "Okay, Mom."

She pushed in her chair and said, "I'm not really hungry. I'm going to go take a bath."

"You sure?" Dad said, watching her with concern. She nodded. "I'll make some tea and bring it in to you," he told her.

As she walked out of the room, I felt tears welling up in my eyes. I'd never seen my mom give up. I thought she was indestructible. Nothing could stop her from making her salon the best around.

Well, I guess nothing except for me.

Dad came over and hugged me. "It's okay, honey. Don't worry about this, it'll all be fine."

"But it's all my fault," I said, wiping the tears from my cheeks. "There has to be something I can do to fix it. Maybe I can talk to Cecilia? Maybe I can start working on the basement—"

"Mickey, listen to me." Dad took me by the shoulders and looked me straight in the eye. "It's going to be fine, okay? Being on the show is a good thing for your mom—it's just stressful right now. But I don't want you getting any more involved in this. This is adult business. Is that understood?"

I nodded yes. I understood. I understood that he

was saying I was the one who'd gotten them into this mess, and if I stayed any more involved I would make things even worse. And I knew it was possible to make a situation even worse because I'd done it before. Some might say it was one of my many talents.

I was too upset and stressed to eat, too, so I went back to my room, shutting the door tight. Maybe I could get swept up in the magic of the gothic South through one of our country's greatest pieces of literature. I opened *TKAM* to the dog-eared page and began reading once again. I only had two short chapters left, but once again, my little mind started drifting . . . to Mom . . . the salon . . . Eve . . . and to Kyle . . . and his hand in mine.

Wait. I sat upright in my bed. That was not what I was supposed to be thinking about. Scratch that and reboot.

I picked up my phone and called Eve. Maybe if I told her about Kyle and hiking I'd understand that it was all nothing. Kyle and I were just friends—nothing else. I also wanted to tell someone what had happened at the salon. If I just talked through it with her, I might come up with a solution. Jonah had helped me before, but I knew Eve could be a great listener, too.

The phone rang and rang until it went to voice

mail. I hung up, feeling even worse. Of course Eve was with Jonah. She was always with Jonah these days. That's why I had been with Kyle in the first place.

I stared at the words on the page of my book, trying to concentrate. Maybe the basement wasn't as bad as we all thought it was. Maybe we really were overreacting and Cecilia would show it simply as a space that needed improving. Maybe everyone would see that I was joking about the mutant zombie rats. Maybe it would all work out without my having to do anything.

The only thing I could do for sure was study and do well on my test.

I picked up my phone and called Eve again. She'd helped Jonah study, so maybe she could help me. But once again it went to voice mail. I slammed the phone down on my bed. My plan to get Eve back together with her friends seemed more important than ever now. That girl needed to get her priorities straight.

I went over to the computer and Googled the book, hoping to come up with some online CliffsNotes to help me study for tomorrow's test. Don't get me wrong, the book wasn't terrible—in fact, I actually liked it. I just didn't have time to finish. I really needed Eve. She was such a good student and with all the *studying* she'd been doing lately, I thought she could help me—and maybe listen to me cry about what I did to the salon.

I called one more time.

"Hello?"

"Eve!" I said, breathing a sigh of relief. "Finally. I've been trying to call you."

"What's wrong?" she asked.

"Everything. It's like, just when you think nothing can go wrong, *wa-paw*! Something blows up. Remember how awful the basement was where I dyed your hair blue?"

"Only when I have nightmares."

"Well, Cecilia went down there today and saw everything."

"Oh no," she said. "Did she say what she's going to do about it?"

"Other than rope it off with crime-scene tape?" I said. "I'm not sure. Mom finds out tomorrow. That's when Cecilia's going to make her recommendations. I think that's why Mom is so upset tonight—"

The phone beeped, and Eve said, "Oops, sorry, Mick. That's the other line. Hang on a sec."

Eve clicked over and the line went silent. At least I finally got her on the phone. Once I talked things out with her, I knew I'd feel much better about everything that was happening. I waited, thinking about the verdict Cecilia might lay down tomorrow.

Maybe I was right. Maybe Mom was just so nervous that she was getting all worked up about something that really wasn't that big of a deal. If she thought of the basement as a style makeover like I'd said, she'd see it wasn't an impossible job.

I held the phone in the crook of my neck and flipped through the pages of my book. Ms. Carlisle gave us study sheets but I'd left mine at school. Of course I had, because nothing in my life could go right.

I started reading again as I waited for Eve. I had gone through several pages when I realized she still hadn't clicked back over from the other line. I'd been waiting for close to ten minutes now.

I hung up, then called her back, withholding judgment until she gave me an explanation. When she answered I said, "Hello? Did you forget you had someone else on the other line?"

"Oh my gosh, I'm so sorry. I'm talking to Jonah. He has this English test tomorrow, too. I was just helping him out."

"I thought you guys already studied this afternoon?"

"We did," she said. "But now he has more questions. I better get back to him. But we'll talk tomorrow, okay? I want to hear all about the thing with Cecilia."

"Yeah, okay," I said quietly. "See you tomorrow."

I hung up feeling incredibly hurt. I'd just been ditched. Well, first I was forgotten about and then I was ditched. Talk about feeling like a loser.

If Eve wanted to have Jonah as her boyfriend and hang out with him once in a while, that was one thing. But to completely ignore your friends again and again . . . to forget all about them? Kyle and I really needed to save them both from that heinous thing they called a relationship.

It wasn't until I picked my book up again that I remembered I had called her for help with the test, too. But I guess it didn't matter. She had already chosen Jonah over me. It was like she'd decided her world had to revolve around him. Like she didn't need anyone else. Including me.

CHAPTER 12

The next morning, Jonah came in the back door just as I headed out the front.

"Mickey! Wait up!" he called. I shut the front door and started walking.

Immature move? Maybe. But I was tired and running late for school because I'd been up late studying. Alone. Hopefully I'd actually remember what I'd read when it came time to take the test.

Moments later the front door opened and I could hear Jonah running down the sidewalk after me.

"Hey, what's up with you?" he asked when he caught up.

"Nothing."

"Oh, man!" he said. "I'm so going to bomb my English test today. My dad said he didn't read *To Kill a Mockingbird* until college, but we're expected to read it now? Come on. Did you know it's the only book that author wrote? He never wrote another one."

"*She,*" I said, annoyed that he didn't know. Hadn't he and Eve spent all night talking about this book? "And her name is Harper Lee."

"Right," he said. We walked a few more paces in silence. Then he asked, "You okay? You're acting funny."

"I'm fine. I'm just tired."

"Man, me too," he said. "I'm pretty stressed about this test."

We turned toward the school and I said, "Jonah, I have the same test today. I'm stressed, too. And *I* didn't have a study partner."

"Hey, sorry, Mickey," he said, looking taken aback. "I guess I forgot." He shrugged.

My head almost exploded with anger on that last word—*forgot.*

"Clearly," I said, and walked off, leaving him behind.

On my way to class I heard footsteps coming up behind me. Kristen and Lizbeth landed on either side of me, grabbing my arms.

"Sheesh, you guys," I said. "What's going on?"

"That's what we're here to find out," Kristen said. She gently brushed her long bangs off her face but kept them dangling outside the red flower headband she wore. "So tell us *everything.*"

"About what?"

"About *Kyyyyyyle*," she said, dragging his name out.

"We heard you guys went out yesterday," Lizbeth said. "So are you together now?"

"No!" I said quickly. "At least not like you mean. How did you hear about it, anyway?"

"Cara Fredericks was with her mom at Hello, Gorgeous! and saw you two drop off your bags," Lizbeth said. "She said it looked like you were getting pretty chummy, if you know what I mean." She nudged my shoulder with hers.

"We didn't go out," I said. "We went hiking. Big difference."

"Oh, please," Kristen said. "You two were alone in the woods. Tell us about it!"

"We hiked."

"And . . . ?" Kristen said.

"And there's a killer view at the top of the mountain."

I thought of how Kyle looked, gazing out at our town, and how sweet he was for taking me up in the first place. Wait. Why was I thinking about Kyle like that? I was seriously wishing that Eve and I had had a chance to talk last night. Something was going on that I needed to figure out.

"Did you watch the sunset together?" Lizbeth asked. "Because if you watched the sunset, then *that* is a full-on date." I looked at her closely. She was experimenting with green eye shadow and I couldn't say it looked good.

"We didn't watch the sunset," I said. It had set at some point, but we didn't exactly sit up there and watch it go down.

"It sounds like a great place to do that. Hey, K," Lizbeth said as we turned down the hall. "Should we ask the guys to take us up there sometime?"

"Views overlooking the city with a possible sunset?" she said. "Definitely."

"Just so you know," I said, "there's a lot of climbing to get up there."

"Climbing?" Lizbeth asked.

"Yeah. The kind where you have to pull yourself up on the rocks to get to the top. I almost slipped at one point." I left out the part where it was just a small part of the climb. And that Kyle had helped me a tiny bit. With his bare hand . . . holding mine.

As if Kristen could actually read my thoughts, she asked, "Please tell me Kyle at least tried to hold your hand."

"Or you held his?" Lizbeth added, her eyes brightening.

I felt my face turn a deep red. I had to stop all these questions before I started to sweat with nerves like I had yesterday. Besides, why did hanging out with a guy have to mean *everything*? No one ever teased me when Jonah and I used to hang out.

Key words there—*used to*.

"Listen, before I head off to class, what are you guys doing tonight?" I asked.

"Unfortunately, nothing," Lizbeth said. "Why? Should we all do something together?"

"Oh yes!" Kristen said. "All six of us! Eight if Eve and Jonah want to come."

"No," I said a bit too firmly. "I mean, let's just have it be us girls. We can go see a movie or something. We can meet at the salon since I have to work for a couple of hours after school. Say, seven?"

"Sounds good to me," Lizbeth said.

Kristen reluctantly agreed. "Maybe we can at least tell the guys what we're doing and then drop hints that they should come by the theater?" she suggested. "That way we can innocently run into them and then *poof*! We're all at the movies on a Friday night."

"Maybe," I said, trying to maintain cool and not scream, *No boys allowed!* "But it has been a while since just us girls hung out. It might be fun to go boyless for one night."

"That's true," Lizbeth said. "That way we can actually relax and not worry about strategy every second."

"And you won't have to obsess about what to

wear," Kristen said to her. "Like that green eye shadow you've got going on there."

"What's wrong with my shadow?" Lizbeth asked, looking at us both.

I tried to be gentle when I said, "Well, I'm just not sure that particular shade goes with the color of your eyes."

"Or your skin," Kristen blurted out. "Or your hair color."

"Great, thanks a lot," Lizbeth said. "Come on, Kristen. Come with me to the bathroom so I can wipe it off?"

"Oh, now I feel bad," I said. Because I did. But for real, the color looked like mushy green peas were coating her lids. "We'll find you a color tonight that's perfect on you, okay?"

"Fine," she said. She tugged on Kristen's arm and shaded her eyes with her other hand.

"See you at lunch," Kristen said as Lizbeth practically dragged her down the hall.

"See you, guys," I called out.

Finally, my plan for getting Eve Jonah-free for a night was up and running. By the end of the weekend I'd have her completely reformed. No way could a night out with Jonah be better than hanging out with her three best friends. She'd see.

CHAPTER 13

When I walked into the cafeteria for lunch, I spotted Eve sitting alone at the table. I looked around and saw that Kristen and Lizbeth were sitting at the boys' table again. Oh well. I guess since they'd have to pull themselves away from the guys for the night, it didn't matter that they'd ditched us for lunch.

Walking toward our usual table, I tried to catch eyes with the girls. They never looked my way. They were so buried in giggling convo that they wouldn't have noticed a fire drill.

"Hey," I said, sitting down beside Eve. "Where are Jonah and Kyle?"

Say detention! I thought.

"Hey, Mick," she smiled. Nodding behind her, she said, "They're in line."

I looked over and saw them picking out sides for their lunches. I didn't have a lot of time before they came over, and I couldn't ask her to abandon Jonah on a Friday night in front of him. He'd probably remind her that she'd lost some new bet in which she had to take him to dinner at Antonio's.

"So!" I said brightly as I took a fruit salad out of my lunch bag. I wanted to tell her how hurt I was at being ignored again yesterday, but decided that I should instead concentrate on moving forward with my and Kyle's plan. If we were successful, I wouldn't have to worry about her ditching me like that anymore. "We're all meeting at the salon at seven tonight for a girls' night. We're going to the mall to see a movie and then do some shopping at Sephora. Poor Lizbeth made the tragic mistake of wearing green eye shadow. Next thing you know she'll be curling her bangs!"

"Sounds fun," she said. "Hope you guys have a good time."

"Want to come with us?" I asked. I wiggled my eyebrows up and down, hoping she'd get the hint that she *should* come with us.

"I can't," she replied. "Jonah and I have plans." A grin flickered across her face, which should have told me this was hopeless, but I had to keep trying.

"What could you guys possibly be doing that's more important than finding the perfect shadow for Lizbeth?"

"We're going roller-skating," she said, now with a

full-on smile. And, I noticed as I peered more closely at her, a slight blush.

"Roller-skating?"

"I know it's random."

"Completely."

"But I'm really excited. And you have to admit—roller-skating is fun."

I didn't want to admit anything right then—especially defeat. I tried another approach—guilt. "The thing is, we all haven't been out just the four of us in a long time. Everyone's getting so crazy over boys that I think it's important that we take time to remember our friends. Don't you think? It'll be like a sisterhood bonding thing."

"Speaking of boys," she said, turning to me with a glance toward the lunch line. "How'd it go with Kyle yesterday?"

My stomach sank. I'd wanted to talk to her about that, but not *now*, in the caf as Kyle and Jonah walked over to us.

"It was fine," I said. "But really, think about tonight because we're going to—"

"Eve, explain to Kyle the awesomeness of level seven," Jonah interrupted. He plopped his lunch tray next to Eve's and sat down. Kyle sat across from me.

"Level seven of what?" I asked.

"Alien Doom," Jonah said, leaning around Eve to tell me.

I felt my throat go dry. I knew Eve liked to play video games with Jonah, but *I* used to be Jonah's main competitor. They were doing *everything* together. Jonah hadn't even invited me over to play video games in forever.

"I only made it that far because you showed me the trick," Eve said.

And now he was showing her the secrets to the game? He'd never do that for me! I had to put a stop to this, and now. I had to think fast, get her distracted, separate those two so I could ambush one of them. If I couldn't get Eve alone now maybe I could work on Jonah, using Kyle as backup. I looked at my water bottle and thought of lunch the other day, when Eve accidentally knocked it all over me.

I took a sip from the bottle, then set it down on the table near Eve. Then I innocently reached for a chip and—oops!—hit the bottle instead, sending it all down Eve's shirt and pants.

"Oh my gosh!" I said. "Eve, I'm so sorry!"

Eve gasped, looking down at her pale pink jeans, now darkened with the water soaking through them and the ends of her loose white top. "Oh no," she said. "I need napkins!"

"You need paper towels," I said, trying to blot her with my one measly napkin. "You better head to the bathroom."

"Yeah, you're right," she said, standing up.

As she walked out—wet spot on her butt and all—Jonah said, "Smooth going, Mickey."

I swatted his arm.

"Hey!" he said, grabbing his arm. "What's that for?"

"Sorry," I said, checking to make sure Eve was out of earshot. "Could you guys go one night without seeing each other?"

"Yes, we could," he said, eyeing me warily. "But we're going out tonight."

"I can't believe you two," I said, then sent a meaningful look in Kyle's direction. *Dude, help a girl out!*

"Yeah," Kyle chimed in. "If you want, we can hang out tonight. Hit up the arcade—we haven't done that in a while."

"Eve and I have plans," Jonah said again.

"Doing what?" Kyle asked.

Jonah hesitated before saying to Kyle, "We're going skating."

"As in boarding?"

"As in roller," Jonah said, his face turning red.

Kyle busted out laughing. "What? You can't be serious. Dude, we haven't done that since, like, fifth grade."

"Shut up, man," Jonah said, trying to regain his

dignity. "If you *ever* get a girlfriend I won't make fun of your dates." Then, I swear, Jonah looked at me . . . and then Kyle did, too.

"Listen, Jonah," I said, looking toward the exit to the restrooms. Still clear. "This was your idea, wasn't it? Roller-skating?"

He shrugged. "Yeah. So?"

"Did she act kind of . . . I don't know, weird when you suggested it?"

"How should I know?" he said. "She's a girl. You all act funny. *You've* been acting weird all day."

I looked at Kyle again, his brown eyes piercing into mine. He gave me a look like, "Have you?"

"I have not," I said to Jonah. "Look, Eve wouldn't want me to tell you this, but . . . she has a truly heinous memory of roller-skating. She used to like going until Marla, her best friend at her old school, told her she didn't want to be her friend anymore and ditched her at the roller rink. It's hard enough to have any dignity in a pair of ugly brown boots with orange wheels that a million people before you have worn. But to get dumped in them, too? Now when Eve sees a pair of skates she basically breaks out in hives."

Jonah looked at me skeptically. "Then why'd she say yes?"

"Because!" I said, trying to think of something believable. "She probably panicked. Who wants to tell their boyfriend that they don't like his idea for a date? But I can tell you—she doesn't want to go. It's actually kind of bad that you suggested it. She was totally traumatized."

Jonah looked over at the exit. "Oh," he said. "I don't want her to feel bad."

I nodded. "Don't say anything to her—especially in front us. Just, like, text her or something that you don't want to go anymore. Really, you'll be doing her a favor."

"Maybe we can do something else," he suggested hopefully.

"Jonah, have you not been listening?" I said. "Unless you come up with something *big* to do in the next few hours, you better just postpone. Seriously, you don't want to suggest another major fail like roller-skating. I'm telling you, Eve's really upset—she just hides it well."

Jonah considered this.

"Dude, we can do something," Kyle piped in. "Let's hit the skate park after school, then check out the new games at the arcade in the mall."

"I don't—"

"Hi, Eve!" I said as she came back to the table.

"Uh, hi, guys," she said, looking at me suspiciously as she sat down. Her pants were sort of dry but, um, not really. It was an improvement, though. "Were you guys just talking about me?" She looked between the three of us. The three of us looked at one another.

"Oh my gosh, Eve!" I said suddenly. "Our test! It's next period. We should go study, right?"

"Jonah said it wasn't that hard," Eve said. She gave me a weird look. "Are you okay, Mickey?"

"Of course!" I replied. "I just didn't have a study partner last night so if you wouldn't mind helping me out now?" Really, I knew I was laying it on thick. "Come on, Eve. We can do a quick cram session." I gathered up my stuff. Eve shrugged and then grabbed her stuff, too.

"Probably a good idea," she said. "You guys are too weird today."

I smiled as we walked out of the cafeteria. Score one for team Mickey and Kyle.

CHAPTER 14

"I finished the book but didn't get what Boo Radley's deal was," I said to Eve. "Was that symbolism or something?"

Eve and I sat in the empty halls near our English class, leaning against the lockers.

"I think he represents, like, the good in people, no matter what they've been through," she replied.

"Right," I said, writing it down. "The good in people." Like the greater good of me helping Eve and Jonah see that their friends were important, too.

"Jonah said on the test we have to name two things Boo represents. We get a bonus for three. So the good in people is one," she said. "And I think he also has something to do with Scout's growth. Or maybe maturity? Because at the end she's not afraid of him and even likes him, like she—" Eve's phone beeped, indicating a new text had come in. She dug it out of her bag. "Like she sees him as not scary anymore." Her brow furrowed as she read the text.

"You okay?" I asked.

She shook her head, staring at the phone. She started to text something back, then stopped. "I think Jonah just canceled on me for tonight."

"What'd he say?" I asked.

She held up the phone for me to read:

Forget roller-skating. Sorry I suggested it!!!

"What's that about?" she asked, looking back at the screen.

"Weird," I said. "But Jonah and Kyle were talking at lunch about hanging out since they haven't in so long. They mentioned the skate park and arcade."

"Really?" She looked up at me. Her wispy hair fell over her eyes but she didn't brush it aside; she just let it hang there. "So he just bailed?"

I felt my stomach start to clench. I didn't want Eve to be sad or upset but I had to stick to the plan—because the plan would fix everything.

She started texting back.

"What are you writing?"

When she finished she said, "I just wrote, 'Okay, never mind I guess. I'll just hang with the girls.' If that's still cool with you?"

"Of course!" I said. "You're always invited."

"Thanks, Mickey," she said. She chucked her phone back in her bag, then sat quietly, flipping through her notes.

"I'm really sorry, Eve," I said. Having my friend miserable was not part of the plan.

"It's stupid," she said.

"What do you mean?"

"It's just that tonight was kind of a big deal."

"Really?" I asked.

"Yeah. Not because of roller-skating or anything dumb like that. Even though I was excited about it. I mean, when was the last time we went roller-skating? Like, fifth grade. I thought it would be fun."

"I'm sure it would have been," I said, starting to feel really bad. But we would have fun tonight, too. I promised myself that I would make sure Eve had the best night with her friends ever.

"Tonight was going to be my first date," she admitted. "My mom said you always remember your first date, and now this is what I'll remember from mine."

"What about Monday afternoon?" I asked. "Wasn't that a date? Ice cream and dinner and a game?"

"No, not exactly," she said. "All that just sort of happened. Except for the ice cream. That was planned. Something about tonight felt more official."

"Oh, Eve," I said. What had I done? "I'm sure Jonah

didn't do it to be mean. He's just a boy, you know?"

She shifted her body to face me. "Yeah, but you know Jonah. It doesn't seem like him to bail like this, does it?" She looked at me hopefully. I gulped.

"I'm sure there's a good reason," I said. Yeah. Me. Could I feel any worse? "But we'll have a blast tonight. I'm going to buy you everything at the concession stand, okay?"

She forced a smile. "Thanks, Mickey. You're a good friend."

CHAPTER 15

The buzz and energy in Hello, Gorgeous! was at an all-time high on Friday afternoon. I was practically run over by stylists, clients, cameras, and a bunch of new people dressed in all black who I didn't recognize: the Head Honchos.

"It's crazy in here," I said to Megan. She had the phone resting on her shoulder while she looked something up on the computer. "What can I do?" I asked.

"I'm so glad you're here," she said. "We can totally use the help."

I looked around and realized the energy was high but not happy. Everyone looked frazzled.

"Cecilia's 'experts,'" Megan said, making quotes with her fingers when she said *experts*, "are observing us before Cecilia makes her recommendations. They're supposed to just watch, and maybe give little tips here and there, but everyone's feeling the pressure. No one wants to be criticized on TV."

I watched Giancarlo, his hand on his hip as his "expert" showed him something with the scissors.

"So she hasn't made her recommendations yet?" I asked.

"No, but those Honchos are causing enough grief for now. Giancarlo's guy is some supposed big shot from Chicago. Award-winning this-or-that," she said. "I didn't catch the details." We looked at Giancarlo and I could tell he was holding in a load of frustration as his Head Honcho hovered nearby.

Megan looked me over and said, "You better get changed before you-know-who sees you and shames you on camera for not wearing your uniform."

"I'm already being shamed on camera for wearing it," I said.

As I walked to the back, several of the Head Honchos stood beside our stylists' chairs, watching them closely and giving advice.

"That is not how I do it," Giancarlo said to a short young man with James Dean hair.

"But that's my point," the man said. "The way you're doing it leaves bad angles."

"Boy, I have been doing hair for twenty years. I don't need some kid to—"

"Again, that's my point!" the guy said. "You've

been doing it one way for so long that you don't even know about the new techniques! If you'd just listen . . ."

I kept walking to the back. I didn't want to see a throwdown.

"Hello, Mickey," Mom said. Not exactly a warm greeting but at least she hadn't banished me from the salon. She followed me into the break room carrying an armful of shampoos and conditioners.

"Is everything okay?" I asked. "I mean, with the Head Honchos being here, watching all the stylists?"

She set the bottles on the table. "It's fine."

"I think Giancarlo is about to ultimate-fight with his assistant," I said.

"I think everyone is really learning a lot," she said. But I could tell from the tone of her voice that she knew there was a very real possibility of a brawl. "How was your English test today?"

"It was fine," I said. "I think I did pretty well." There had been an essay question about friendship, and how it relates to Boo Radley. I'd thought for a while on that, tapping my pen nervously on my desk. I thought of Eve, and how open and nice she always was—always real—and how that attitude made it easy to become friends with her. Eve's no Boo, but it made me see that simple kindness can lead to friendship, as Scout learned at the end of the book when she was faced with ol' Boo.

"That's great," she said, and something about her attitude seemed too casual.

"You seem more . . . relaxed since last night," I said, nervous about bringing it up. I've learned that it's best not to remind people of the pain and anguish you've caused them.

"Everything is going to be fine," she said, though her voice was a bit forced. She made room on the shelf and placed the bottles she'd brought up one by one. "The stylists are getting some help from the assistants but I'm sure they could still use a hand and a sweep. And don't forget Rowan. See if she needs anything, too."

"You got it," I said.

I put on my smock and got to work. I started by sweeping Violet's station. She was the calmest of the stylists today, but I guess she had to set a good example, being the manager and all.

"Make sure those layers don't create a shelf in the back of her head," the Head Honcho directed.

"I won't," Violet said calmly. Though I could see a look of panic in her eyes.

This had probably already been a long day for everyone.

A little later, Giancarlo asked me to *please* go get him a bottle of water from the back. He looked wiped. "And get me the sparkling, not the flat," he said. "And chilled, not warm."

Because it was Giancarlo I didn't mind the terse tone of his voice—I knew he didn't mean it.

I got a small chilled bottle from the back, then started back up to the floor. As I passed the basement door, I thought I heard something, someone talking down there, but I wasn't sure. I paused to listen. Suddenly, the door went flying open and I stumbled back away from it. Cecilia busted through, slamming the door behind her.

"Mickey," she said with a smile. Her black cat's-eye glasses were looking a little dusty on the lenses but her red hair still held its springy curl. "Good to see you again. How's the work going?"

"Fine! Everything's great."

"That's good." She smiled, wiping her hands on a towel. It was already covered in dirt. "The team is very lucky to have you here."

"So, uh . . . what's happening down there?" I asked, trying to seem like I was just making friendly conversation.

"We're just looking at our options," she said. "Have you found any more of those great vintage hair clips?" I couldn't believe she'd remembered that from her first day here. She really did care about what I said and did.

"No, not recently," I said.

"If you do, be sure to show me," she said. "I do love vintage."

"Me too!" I said. "And, um, I'll show you if I find anything."

Cecilia went out to the floor to check on her Head Honchos and I followed behind to deliver Giancarlo's chilled, sparkling water. He was still red-faced over his Head Honcho's *suggestions* (although I heard him use the word *demands*), but when he saw Cecilia he took a deep breath and continued cutting. I cautiously set the water on his station and backed away.

Devon was going through something similar with her Head Honcho—an older woman who called her technique "old-fashioned and in big need of an update." Of course Devon took great offense to this since she specialized in retro looks. But everyone managed to keep their mouths shut and just do the work. Mom wouldn't have it any other way.

Kristen and Lizbeth showed up at six thirty—half an hour early—looking extra fab. I had a feeling it had something to do with the cameras that were turning on them at that very moment.

Clearly they'd gone home and changed after school. Lizbeth wore a studded chambray shirt, her dark hair pulled back, and long, metallic earrings that almost grazed her shoulders. Kristen wore a pink, silver, and black patterned jacket with a short black skirt and a long, layered pink-and-silver necklace.

Lizbeth looked away shyly as the camera focused on them, but Kristen kept her head high and gazed around the salon as if it were her country and she was its queen.

"Hey, you guys," I said. "Early for a reason?"

"Well, Kristen had been talking about doing her nails in neon," Lizbeth began, "and we were meeting you here, anyway, so we just figured, you know." She looked a little guilty and embarrassed.

"Kristen, don't you already have a hair appointment for tomorrow?" I asked her.

"You're the one who asked us to meet here," she said. "Besides, I get easily bored with my color."

"Right," I said and grinned.

When I came back from getting my friends settled at the manicure station with their drinks, I saw that Cecilia and her Head Honchos had left. Mom was at the front telling Megan she had some errands to run and she'd be back in an hour or so, and I realized I missed my chance to ask her about Cecilia's recommendations. I wondered how nervous she was about it.

The entire salon seemed to let out a deep breath once the door closed behind Mom. No more boss, no more Cecilia, and no more Head Honchos.

"Micks, can you do me a favor?" Megan asked. "I'm so hungry but I haven't been able to move since Cecilia and her team got here. Could you watch the front for five minutes while I run next door to CJ's to grab a muffin and some tea?"

"Sure," I said. "Do you know what happened with the recommendations?"

"No idea. Sorry, Mick. You'll have to ask yor mom. There aren't any appointments coming in right now," she said, looking at the schedule on the computer. "So you should be good."

I took my place behind the counter. I liked working reception. It felt a little like being in charge.

"Did the cameras catch you before they left?" I asked Kristen.

"No," she said. She slumped in her chair. "Tomorrow is my last chance. I have to make it count."

While Kristen and Lizbeth were having their nails done, I asked them what they wanted to do tonight. We talked about sneaking into a scary movie, but Lizbeth admitted she was too chicken—of the scary movie and of getting busted.

"Can't we just see that new love-letter movie?" she asked.

"We'll ask Eve when she gets here," I said as the phone rang. "Hello, Gorgeous!" I answered.

"Confirming a delivery for Cecilia von Tressell," a

sharp, businesslike voice said.

"Here? For Cecilia?" I asked.

"We've got the buttercream she ordered. Just confirming the address."

"Oh, right. She's already left but she's staying at . . . ," I said, shuffling through the papers on the desk. What hotel had Cecilia said she'd be staying at? "The Bradford!" I said, suddenly remembering. "She's at the Bradford."

"So we should send this over there?" he asked.

"Yes," I said. "Do you need the address?"

"Nope, we got it," he said. "Have a good night."

I hung up the phone, feeling very professional. "Cecilia must have ordered cupcakes," I told Lizbeth. "Buttercream."

"Yum," Lizbeth said.

My stomach rumbled. Maybe I should jet to CJ's for something sweet when Megan got back.

CHAPTER 16

That night, we all decided to see a romantic comedy, agreeing that if we were going to make it a girls' night, we should go all out. We had an hour before it began, so we hit up Sephora to test the samples and browse the new products.

"Mickey, what do you think?" Lizbeth asked, having just tested a deep green shadow on one eye.

"Better than the light green," I said, peering closely at her. "But still . . . I'd try a dark blue."

She clutched the wand with green power still on the tip. "But the green is calling to me!"

"Eve would look good in the green," I said. "Her skin tone is perfect for it."

I picked up the shadow Lizbeth had been using. "Want me to put this on you?" I asked Eve, reaching for a disposable shadow brush.

Eve took a quick look at the color, then shook her head.

"It'll look so pretty on you," I coaxed. "If you like it I'll buy it for you."

Eve gave me a funny look. "Thanks," she said. "But that's okay." She paused before continuing, "Why are you being so nice to me?"

"Because you're my friend!"

"You can buy me something," Kristen offered, holding a fistful of lip gloss, mascara, and blush. "I have my big debut tomorrow for the cameras. When the opening credits for this episode roll, it's going to say, 'And introducing . . . Kristen Campbell.'"

"I'm sure it will," I told Kristen. "But you're not the one who's down."

When Eve had met us at the salon, her eyes had looked a little sad. She kept checking her phone, too, as we walked to the mall. I knew she was still upset about Jonah, but I wanted her to focus on having fun with us girls.

"What's wrong?" Kristen asked her.

"Nothing," Eve said.

"Something's wrong," Lizbeth said. "Is it Jonah?"

Her face flushed pink and she said, "Who *cares* about Jonah?"

"Um, not you?" Lizbeth said, looking at her carefully.

"Exactly. I'm going to wait outside," she said. She turned and walked out of the store.

The second she was gone, Kristen and Lizbeth dropped their makeup and came up to me.

"What's that about?" Lizbeth asked, looking worried.

"Do we need to hunt down Jonah Goldman and whoop him?" Kristen asked. "Because if he did something to her . . ." She pounded her fist into her hand, which would have been funny if the situation weren't so awful—and avoidable.

A blind person could see how upset Eve had been when she'd gotten Jonah's text. But even worse, I was pretty sure he hadn't planned to totally cancel on her. I'd let her think that. Now Eve was as miserable as I'd ever seen her, and we were all worried about her. This girls' night was not turning out the way I'd planned at all.

"Come on," I said, and we went outside to find her.

Eve was sitting on a bench not far from the store, checking her phone.

Kristen and Lizbeth sat down on either side of her. I hovered nearby. My stomach cramped up, seeing her there so sad, knowing it was all my fault. I started seriously thinking about texting Jonah and asking him to meet us here. I had to do something to fix what I'd done.

"Eve, come on," Lizbeth said gently. "Tell us what's wrong."

She took a deep breath. "It's just that Jonah and I were supposed to go out tonight. Just us. On a date. But he bailed at the last minute and I can't figure out why. He just sent me this text that was like, *Sorry I asked. Later.* I don't get it."

"Well, maybe something came up?" Lizbeth suggested. "Mickey, you're his best friend. Did he say anything to you about Eve or tonight?"

"I—I don't know. I mean, not really." My face began to burn. Great. I'd ruined everything and now I was lying about it. Sometimes I wished there were a how-to guide to being a good friend. How to Not Make Your Best Friend the Most Miserable Person in the World By Lying To Her and How To Fix It If You Do—that was the article I needed at the moment.

Eve looked up from her phone and said, "You told me he said he had plans with Kyle."

"Yeah," I said. I really didn't want to lie anymore. But now I felt stuck. "He did—he said something like that. Kyle said something, too."

Eve held my gaze for a moment as if I might say more. But I didn't.

"I don't like Jonah upsetting you, no matter what the reason," Lizbeth said. She rubbed Eve's back, a sweet gesture I wished I'd thought to do.

"He's a jerk," Kristen said.

"No, he's not," I said quickly. They looked at me like I'd just betrayed Eve, so I added, "I just mean, I'm sure there's a good reason. One we don't know yet."

"Whatever," Kristen said, unconvinced. "He better run and hide if he sees me coming, that's all I'm saying."

"Thanks, you guys," Eve said. "Sorry I'm being such a downer. I really am glad we planned tonight. It's been a while since we've hung out, just the girls."

"Your friends will always stick by you when the boys don't," Kristen said, the spokeswoman for Girl Power.

"Maybe we should head toward the theater," Lizbeth said. "We can distract ourselves with popcorn and previews."

We gathered up our bags and headed toward the theater. On the way, we passed by the arcade. There, at the front near the door, I saw the one person I wanted to avoid. Jonah was playing a hunting game with Kyle, shooting at the screen with laser guns.

I wasn't sure what to do.

If Eve and Jonah saw each other, nothing good would come of that.

Jonah was concentrating on the game, which meant he wouldn't see her as we walked by. I had to make sure Eve didn't see him. Otherwise this whole thing—including my friendships—would blow up in my face.

"Have you guys ever been to that store?" I asked, pointing in the opposite direction of the arcade.

"Yeah, Mickey," Kristen said. "We shop there all the time—preparing for our retirement." She laughed.

I looked at where my finger was pointing. The only store in the vicinity was a place that sold orthopedic shoes and elastic-waist pants, and only in black, beige, or white.

"It's actually kind of cool," I said, feeling the sweat gather on my upper lip. We were walking closer and closer to the arcade. "The stuff there is really, um, comfortable."

"Hey!" a voice called. "Eve!"

The girls all turned back toward the voice. I tried to keep walking, but nobody followed.

"Jonah?" Eve said.

"Hey, *Jonah*," Kristen said, folding her arms and stalking toward him. "We were just talking about you."

"Really?" he said, looking nervously between her and Eve.

Eve wouldn't look at him. She kept her eyes focused firmly on the floor.

"Yes, we were," Kristen said. She was ready to fight. This was not going to go well.

"Hey, guys!" I said as brightly as I could. "We're on

our way to see *Letters of the Heart*. You can come if you want." Like they'd ever step foot in a theater showing a movie like that? No way. "We better go—it's starting soon!"

"We have, like, half an hour," Lizbeth reminded me.

"Popcorn and all that," I tried.

"Yeah, don't let us keep you," Kyle said. "You guys have fun." He looked at me and shrugged. I knew he was trying to help and I tried to give him a grateful look back.

"Maybe we should go," Kristen said. "Because when *we* make plans, *we* don't break them. Come on, Eve."

Kristen started to tug Eve away but Eve, who looked mad and confused and sad all at once, finally looked Jonah in the eyes. She looked like she was about to say something but couldn't decide where to begin.

"Wait," Jonah said. "Do you maybe want to meet up after the movie? In the food court or something?" He looked at Eve, then he looked at all of us.

"Jonah, no one—" Kristen began.

"Kristen," I interrupted. "Don't." But she was already off and running.

"You had your chance to hang out with Eve. You can't cancel on her and then still hang out with her. That's not cool."

Jonah's brow furrowed. "Cancel? I didn't cancel," he said.

"We saw the text," she replied.

Eve finally spoke. "I showed them because I was upset. You don't just bail on someone you have plans with."

All I could think was, *Oh my gosh. This is really happening.*

"I *didn't* bail," Jonah said. "You did."

"What?" Eve said, almost laughing. She quickly pulled her phone out of her pocket and opened her texts. "Then what's this about?" She scrolled through old messages before reciting: " 'Forget roller-skating. Sorry I suggested it.' "

Jonah's eyes bulged out of his head. "What about *your* text back to *me*?" He scrambled to get his own phone about of his pocket, then read aloud. " 'Okay, never mind I guess. I'll just hang with the girls.' *That* is canceling."

"Because you already had!" Eve said.

"No, I didn't," Jonah said. "I just said forget roller-skating."

"Yeah, but by then you'd already made plans with Kyle to hang out. And why did you say forget roller-skating, anyway?"

"I hadn't made plans with Kyle," Jonah explained as I seriously started to sweat. "I had plans with you. And I canceled skating because of—" He paused, lowering his voice. "Because I didn't know it had such bad memories for you."

Aww. Jonah really was a sweet guy. His tone made me realize how much he cared for Eve. And that made me the worst friend in the whole world.

"Bad memories?" Eve asked. "What are you talking about?"

"Your old best friend? And the fight you had?" he said. "And what made you think I already had plans with Kyle?"

I felt like I was going vomit. Or maybe pass out. I definitely couldn't move.

"What fight are you talking about?" Eve asked. "Mickey told me that you—"

That's when everything went into hyperfocus. Technicolor. All on me.

"Wait," Eve said, turning to face me. "What's going on?"

"Hmm?" I said as if I'd just popped in the conversation. "What's that?"

"What is this roller-skating story?" she demanded.

"Um, well . . ."

"And why did you tell her I already had plans with Kyle?" Jonah asked.

"See, I . . ."

"It was my idea." We all turned to look at Kyle, who stepped up beside me. "I told Mickey we had plans, and I guess she told Eve. I'm sorry, Jonah. I just thought it'd be cool if we could hang out."

Jonah looked at Kyle for a moment. Then he shook his head. "Dude, that's cool of you to try to step in and all," Jonah said. "But I know Mickey. And this is all her."

"No, it's not," Kyle said. "It was both of our idea. That's the truth."

"This whole roller-skating story?" Jonah said to Kyle. "No way did you come up with that."

Eve glared at me.

"Eve . . . ," I tried.

But she stood rigid, shaking her head the tiniest bit, still a combo of emotions—anger and disbelief. "I can't believe you," she said.

"Look, you guys," I said, my heart racing as I tried to explain. "I promise I didn't mean for it to turn out like this. I swear. I just—well, you've been spending a ton of time together. I just missed you, that's all."

"Save it, Mickey," she said. "You totally tricked us! No, it wasn't a trick. It was a lie. All lies."

"I know!" I said. "I'm so sorry."

Kristen and Lizbeth eyed me and started scooting closer to Eve. Suddenly, all my friends were on one side and Kyle and I were on the other. Them against us.

"Listen, I'm sorry, okay?" I said. "I just wanted us all to hang out together. You have to admit you're all acting a little crazy with this boy stuff." I looked at

Kristen and Lizbeth, too.

"You're one to talk!" Kristen said. She pointed at Kyle.

"We're just friends!" I cried.

"I need to get out of here," Eve said. "Jonah? You want to come with?"

Jonah's eyes pierced through me, full of betrayal. Then he took Eve's hand and they walked away.

CHAPTER 17

"Mickey," Lizbeth said. "Are you insane?"

What a great question. It could be the motto of my life: *Mickey Wilson: Is She Insane?!*

"I'm so sorry about all this," I said to her and Kristen. "I just wanted us all to hang out."

"By lying?" Kristen said. "Mickey, seriously."

"I didn't mean to lie. It was more of a . . . a plan," I said. As soon as I said it, though, I realized how lame it sounded.

"A *plan*?" Lizbeth said.

"Don't just blame Mickey," Kyle said. "It was my idea, too."

"But you didn't know that I was going to tell these stories," I said, turning to him. "About the skating BFF breakup, or letting Eve think Jonah had completely bailed."

"But we both agreed to a plan to get them to spend

some time apart," he said.

He was being really sweet, trying to take some of the blame. But I knew that this was one time I had nothing to share. This was my fault.

"You had no idea how far I'd gone with the plan," I told him.

"Would you two quit bickering about whose fault it is?" Kristen said. "Geez."

"I just don't understand why you did it," Lizbeth said, looking disappointed in us both.

I looked at Kyle, wondering if he had an answer. Something that sounded better than what we'd been giving, which boiled down to us being selfish. I knew our intentions were good, but the execution . . . major fail. All I could say is, "We're sorry."

"You're going to have to do some serious groveling to get Eve to forgive you for this one," Kristen said. "She's so mad she—what *is* it, Lizbeth?"

Lizbeth tugged on the sleeve of Kristen's plum-colored blouse while staring into the arcade. She pointed and said, "They're here."

Kristen turned to look. "Who? Where?" Then she saw what Lizbeth was pointing at.

Matthew and Tobias were waiting in line to get change for the machines.

Kristen started bouncing on the balls of her feet, which set Lizbeth doing the same. "Oh my gosh, oh my gosh, oh my gosh!" they squealed.

"Let's go casually bump into them," Kristen said. "Wait! Should we hit the ladies' room first to freshen up? I think I need more lip gloss."

"Good idea," Lizbeth said. Before they took off, Lizbeth turned to me and said, "Mickey, we get what you were trying to do, but you totally have to talk to Eve and Jonah. Make sure Eve knows that you did it because you missed her or—"

"Come on, they're choosing games," Kristen said, tugging on Lizbeth's arm. "Now's the perfect time."

Lizbeth ran her fingers through her hair. "Text us what happens," she said to me.

"Bye, Kyle!" Kristen said. And then they were gone. Folded into the darkness of the noisy arcade.

That left me standing alone. With Kyle. In the mall on a Friday night.

Which might have been something to get excited about, except that I'd ruined my friendship with Eve and I had a massive amount of damage control to do on Jonah. I wondered if I'd ever repair either friendship. I'd never seen Jonah so mad. And Eve . . . she could barely look at me before she walked away. Tears began stinging my eyes and my nose started to run. Soon, I was crying. In front of Kyle. In the mall, on a Friday night.

"Hey, don't worry, Mickey," Kyle said, trying to

comfort me. "It'll be okay."

"You really think so?" I sniveled. I covered my face with my hands and let it out a bit more.

Kyle stood quietly next to me while I sobbed. Among all the things I'd done, this was the worst. I couldn't believe I ever thought for a single second that it was an okay thing to do.

Finally, I wiped my face and nose as best as I could.

"I'll talk to Jonah tomorrow," Kyle said. "I'm pretty sure they both need some cooling off for the night."

"Agreed," I said, wiping my wet hand on my jeans. The wet smears were tinged with shiny pink, green, and blue makeup. Great. I could use some serious Sephora now to cover up the damage.

"You know what I like to do when I feel like dirt?" Kyle said.

"What?" I asked.

"Eat. Huge amounts of junk food. Like sticky cinnamon buns. Sausage pizza. Seven-layer burrito. And that's just to start. Want to go over to the food court?"

"I don't know," I said.

I thought for a moment. I wasn't even sure I deserved to keep hanging out with Kyle when I messed up my other friendships so bad. But if I had one mini sticky bun, I might feel good enough to begin my plan for fixing things with Jonah and Eve.

"Well," I said, "maybe just a little something."

We started with hot pretzels and Cokes, then quickly headed for hot dogs and pizza. When I pulled my money out of my pocket, Kyle said, "No worries. It's on me."

"Are you sure?" I looked at our trays, piled high with comfort food.

"Yeah," he said. "For successfully completing our mission. Even if we destroyed our friendships in the process."

"When I do something, I do it big," I said, managing a small smile.

We carried our trays back to the table. "I do have a suggestion for the next time we need to help our friends who are dating," I said.

"What's that?" he asked.

"Stay out of it."

"Good plan," he said, and laughed. For a moment, he held my gaze. His soft, wavy curls were getting a tiny bit long, and one was hanging over his forehead. I bit into my pizza, thinking he was a really cute friend. But also knowing that maybe he was becoming more than that.

CHAPTER 18

Kyle's mom picked us up from the mall and drove me home. It was kind of weird sitting alone in the backseat while he sat up front. His mom played light jazz on the radio, and even though it was total old-people music, it was kind of soothing. Nobody spoke, except when his mom asked if we had a good time.

The knot in my stomach over what I'd done grew as I got closer to home. I had to talk to Jonah. This was big—heading toward unforgiveable territory. I knew that the longer I waited, the angrier he'd be and the more likely I'd be to chicken out.

When we pulled up outside my house, I thanked Kyle's mom. Kyle got out with me and we slowly walked to my front door.

"So . . . you're okay?" he asked.

"Yeah. I mean, I guess."

"Want me to talk to Jonah? Maybe break the ice with him?"

I looked down at my phone, clutched in my hand. How long should I wait to call him? "Nah. Thanks, though."

We got to the front door and I realized no one had ever walked me to my door before. In the midst of everything, it was kind of nice.

"I know it wasn't exactly the best of circumstances," Kyle said. He shoved his hands in his pockets and looked down at his shoes. "But I really had a good time tonight. With you." He looked up at me quickly and smiled.

I smiled, too. "Yeah. So did I."

"Is it okay if I text you tomorrow or something?"

I tried to suppress the goofy smile on my face. "Sure."

I watched him leave, waving at him as the car pulled away from the curb.

When I walked into the kitchen, I heard Mom on the phone.

"I understand that. I already went over this with your supervisor. But we need you there tomorrow."

Mom paced back and forth as Dad leaned against the counter and listened. She had on cotton pj bottoms and a silk front-tied blouse, plus the ballet slippers she wore around the house. It looked like she'd been caught in the middle of changing out of her work clothes. I looked at Dad. Their grim faces said something was wrong.

"I don't know what happened," she said, agitated. "I'm trying to fix it. On a tight schedule."

"What's going on?" I asked Dad.

He shook his head, focusing on Mom's call like she was an episode of his favorite TV drama.

"Did Cecilia give her recommendations?" I asked, but he waved me away.

"Yes, in buttercream," Mom said. "Please call back as soon as you know. Thank you."

She ended the call, then put her hand over her eyes. Whatever had just happened, she'd been beat.

"What'd they say?" Dad asked.

"They said it's my problem now. No painters. No paint. How in the world did this happen? What's it going to look like on TV?"

"Something's happening with the show?" I asked. "What's going on?"

"I need to find Cecilia's number," Mom said, rifling through some papers on the table. "I can't believe I'm going to have to call her this late in the evening. I can't believe I'm going to have to call her *at all*."

"Mom?"

She shoved aside the pile of papers and started digging through her bag. "The paints and painters were supposed to come this evening to start work on the basement. That was Cecilia's big recommendation—to renovate the basement. But they never showed and I've been trying to get someone to talk to me all night. The painters not showing threw off the schedule for the flooring, which throws off the schedule for the electrician, which throws the schedule for the delivery of the new equipment . . . everything is off. We don't have any extra time because this all has to be done by six tomorrow evening."

"By six?" I asked. Wow—I knew the schedules were tight, but man.

I'd had so much on my mind, what with ruining friendships and all, but when she mentioned paints, and *buttercream*, I started to think . . .

"Is the name of the paint you're using called buttercream?" I asked Mom.

"Yes," she said.

"Oh." My stomach dropped. Not again.

Mom stopped and looked at me. "Why?"

"It's just that, someone called," I said. "Earlier tonight, when Megan went to CJ's to get some tea. I'm sure it's—"

Mom's phone rang, and she quickly answered it.

"Cecilia! Hello, how are you? Yes, I was just about to call you." Mom paused while Cecilia said something. Her mouth dropped into an *o*.

"There? At your hotel? Oh my . . ." Mom put her hand back over her eyes. "I'm not sure what happened but we're certainly fixing it right now. I'm so sorry you had to call me. Yes. I will. Okay. Good-bye."

Mom hung up and looked at Dad. "You won't believe where the paints ended up," she said.

"Cecilia's hotel," I answered.

Mom turned to me. "How did you know that?"

"That's what I was trying to tell you. There was a call tonight that I didn't think anything about until now. Some guy called about a delivery for Cecilia and I thought he meant *for Cecilia* . . ." Mom watched me carefully as my skin heated up. "I told him what hotel she was at so they could deliver it to her. I thought he was delivering cupcakes," I said, feeling so foolish. "You know, because of the buttercream?"

Mom had a steady look in eyes as she struggled to maintain control. "Megan left you to answer the phone? Where was I?"

"You'd gone to run errands," I said, hoping Megan didn't get in trouble. "She was only gone, like, five minutes, so I worked the desk."

"I should be told about anything that has anything to do with Cecilia, the show, or the salon. Do you not understand that? This is about my business, Mickey."

"I know," I said, feeling shaky. "I'm sorry."

"I need to get to the hotel," she said, tossing things back in her purse.

"I'll go with you," Dad said.

"I'd rather do it alone," she said tersely.

"Chloe, I'm coming with you," Dad insisted.

"Mom, I'm sorry," I said. But she wouldn't look at me. "I didn't know."

She stormed upstairs to get dressed again. It was worse than being yelled at. Way worse.

For the second time in about four hours, I started crying. I covered my eyes like Mom had done, like I had done at the mall, and let it all out. I didn't think I had any tears left, but the tank had been refilled, ready to overflow again.

"Oh, honey," Dad said soothingly, putting his hand on my shoulder. "Calm down, it's okay. Mom and I will take care of it."

"I . . . ruined . . . the show . . . ," I choked through my tears.

"You didn't ruin the show."

"I ruined everything," I sobbed, thinking of all that I had done in just a day. "Everyone hates me."

"No one hates you."

"Eve does," I cried. "Jonah does."

"Why would Jonah hate you?"

"Because," I sniffed, "I told him Eve hates roller-skating."

Dad kind of laughed at that. "I'm sure he's okay with that. Do you want to tell me what's really going on?"

I wiped my nose. Jonah used to be the person I'd

go to when I had problems, but now I had no one. Thinking that made my eyes sting with fresh tears but I forced them back.

"I was upset that Jonah and Eve were together every second of the day," I said. "I thought they'd forgotten who their real friends were. So I just told a little story to keep them from going out together for one night and it all blew up in my face."

Dad dropped his hand from my shoulder and said, "Well, that's usually what happens when you lie."

"I know," I said miserably. "I was stupid to even think to do it. I just have to convince Jonah and Eve that I really am sorry I did it."

"Mickey, I have to say," Dad began, and I knew it wasn't going to be good. "Your mom and I did not raise you to lie. Do you know what would happen if you lied to one of us?" I looked up at him through my tears. "We'd ground you for about a month, and that's just for starters. Lying is not something we tolerate."

"I know," I said quietly.

"Haven't you and Eve had some issues recently?" he asked. I nodded. That was putting it lightly. "All I can say is it sounds like you have a lot of work to do."

I nodded again. I couldn't even speak.

Dad and Mom left to go get the paints. I sat in the kitchen thinking about what to do next. Should I go to work tomorrow? Would Mom even want me there?

I wasn't sure, but I knew that after all I'd done lately it was time I start figuring things out on my own.

So I made a decision: I would go to work and help Mom as best as I could. And I would help by doing something to fix the damage I'd created.

As for Eve and Jonah, I'd do absolutely whatever it took to get them to trust me again. I started by sending Jonah a text:

Can I talk to you? Your porch in 5? Please?

I waited anxiously for a response—anything, just a single word from him to know how he was feeling toward me. Moments later, I got exactly one word back:

Kay.

Before I could even walk up to the back door, Jonah stepped out. I couldn't tell if he was glaring at me, or squinting through the porch lights.

"Hey," he said, shutting the door behind him, like he didn't even want me coming in his house.

"Hey," I said. He sat down on one of the chaise longue chairs on the deck. I sat across from him.

He leaned forward, resting his forearms on his knees. He laced his fingers together, and with his eyes on them said, "Dude, seriously."

"I know—"

"This is so not cool."

"I know—"

He looked up at me, his cowlick mushed flat on his hairline, just like it always did. "Are you jealous that I've been hanging out with Eve?"

"No!" I said, the words flying out of my mouth before I had a chance to think about it. "Why would I be jealous? My two favorite people are together!"

"We were talking about it," he said, "and we both realized that you don't act like you're happy about it. You act like you're pretty mad about it."

They were talking about me? My two best friends were talking about me? I hadn't expected that to happen when they got together. And I wasn't sure I liked it at all.

"I told you," I said, feeling desperate. "I just missed Eve and hanging out with the girls."

"Meanwhile you're hanging out with Kyle," Jonah pointed out.

"We're just friends."

"Tell him that."

We sat silently, staring each other down. I couldn't deal with that now, not that I wanted to. Jonah—and Eve—were more important.

"I just want you to know that I'm sorry," I said. "I didn't mean to interfere. I didn't want to get you

and Eve into such a big misunderstanding, that's for sure."
Jonah didn't say anything, he just kept his eyes on his still-laced fingers. "What are you going to do about Kyle?"

"I texted him earlier," Jonah said. "We're meeting up tomorrow."

I perked up. "You guys are cool again?"

"I'll see what he has to say, just like I'm doing with you."

My shoulders sank. This was harder than I'd thought it would be. And I still had to apologize to Eve, as well.

"But even if I forgive him," Jonah said, "it's different with you."

"Why?" I asked. "Because he's a guy?"

"No," Jonah said, annoyed. He stood up. "Because he's not my best friend. You are."

I stood up, too. What did he mean, "You are"? Like, maybe we could get past this latest mistake?

"Eve really needs to hear from you," he said, his hand on the back door. "Okay?"

I nodded. "I know."

Jonah looked at me one last time before opening the door and going inside, leaving me standing alone on his porch.

Before I left, I dialed Eve's number. Do not pass go, do not bother texting, just go straight to the phone call. It was the next best thing to showing up at her door.

Of course, it went straight to voice mail. I was sure

she was screening my calls.

"Eve," I said when I heard the beep. "I'm mortified. I'm so sorry about what I did, honestly. I didn't mean for you and Jonah to get in a fight. I just . . . it was stupid of me, okay? The truth is . . . maybe I was a little jealous of all the time you two were spending together. I don't know. Maybe I'm also confused about my own feelings for Kyle, which I've been wanting to talk to you about but haven't had a chance because you've been so busy . . ." I knocked my head with the heel of my hand. That was not relevant! "That's not what I mean. I just mean—"

The voice mail beeped, cutting off my terrible speech. I called again.

"Sorry," I said. "Again. I didn't mean that it's your fault for not being around to talk about Kyle—who I have nothing going on with! Oh, shoot. This is the worst apology ever. What I did has nothing to do with anyone but me. And I'm really sorry, Eve. I hope you'll call me back because I really want to tell you in person and not over some recording. Okay? Please? Okay. Bye."

I hung up the phone, wondering if I'd just made things even worse.

I sent off a quick text for good measure:

Just left you vm. Pls listen. I'm so sorry!!!!

Then I went home.

CHAPTER 19

I woke up early Saturday morning, the orange-gold sun shining through my open curtains. My first thoughts were of Kyle and of him standing in the mall with me, looking pretty cute in a dark blue T-shirt and dark jeans. As soon as I pictured the mall, I pictured Eve, then Jonah and the rest of my friends.

My friends. I wondered if any of them still were.

Then I thought about Hello, Gorgeous! I wondered if Mom would have a salon left after today. I'd come up with a plan as I'd drifted off to sleep last night. Now I had to put it into action.

I had to start my day—even this early—with Jonah. Above everyone else, he was the most important.

I texted him a pleading message for the second time in eight hours:

Wake up! Semi emergency! Meet in your yard. Please!

I splashed some water on my face and brushed my teeth. Then I gently ran a comb through my curled and slightly frizzed hair, tossed on some clothes, and headed out.

It was still so early that the grass was covered in dew, cooling my bare feet, and the air smelled extra fresh and clean. With the sun rising in the clear sky, it was going to be a beautiful day.

Just as I shut the gate between our houses, Jonah came out his back door in a gray T-shirt and old gym shorts. His hair stuck up in all directions and he rubbed his eyes against the morning sun.

"You must really want me to hate you," he said. "It's, like, six thirty or something."

"I know, I'm sorry," I said, stepping up on the back porch. We sat back down on the chaise chairs, just like last night.

He gave a noisy yawn. "Are you here to grovel some more?"

"Yes," I said. "And then some."

"Maybe I should just give in now so I can go back to bed." He looked at me and gave me the tiniest of smiles.

"Let me just get this out first, okay?"

"And then I can go back to bed?"

"Well," I said. "Just, listen." He laid back on the chair, getting comfortable. "You have no idea how horrible I feel about what I did to you and Eve, and telling you that story about her and roller-skating."

"Did she and that Marla girl at least have a fight while roller-skating?" he asked. I shook my head no. "Not even a small disagreement?"

"No," I said. "I know they've drifted apart since she moved here, but I don't know of any blowup fights."

"Man, Mickey," he said.

"I know! I guess I just got so focused on how Eve and I had started becoming good friends, but then suddenly we weren't and I wanted to blame you for that. This is all my fault and I want you to know that I'm really going to be different and I'm so sorry for this whole mess."

"Mickey, I forgive you but you gotta pull it together. Don't be so insecure. You have all these new friends—who aren't half-bad, even Kristen. And I'm just going to tell you this once—Kyle likes you. So do whatever you want with that."

I ignored that last statement. I couldn't think about Kyle just then. "You promise you're not mad anymore?"

"I promise. But don't push it." He smiled again. I knew we weren't back to normal yet, but we were on the way and that was good enough for me. "Now can I go back to bed?" He sat up from the lounge chair.

"Actually," I said, "there's one more thing."

He plopped back down. "What?"

"Mom's salon."

"Did you finally burn the place down?"

"Not even funny," I said. "But I did create a bit of a misunderstanding yesterday that has the whole renovation project for the show in trouble. I really need everyone's help."

"Everyone like me?"

"And Kristen and Lizbeth . . ."

"And Kyle," he said and grinned. "I'm in."

And that was a true friend.

The plan was to help Mom get the renovations back on schedule to make sure Mom had a great unveiling on *Cecilia's Best Tressed*. I would get as many people down in the basement as possible to start painting. But we had to get moving. That six-o'clock deadline was going to hit us fast.

I woke Dad up and ran the idea by him. He thought it sounded like a plan that just might work. I raced down to the kitchen and I tried to brew coffee for him. It smelled like burnt tires.

"We got the paints last night, and it's a lot," Dad said, pouring my coffee down the sink, the steam from it washing over his face. He tried not to cringe as the smell hit him. "I know she's still trying to get the painters to come back, but nothing yet." He got the coffee canister from the freezer and measured out scoops for a fresh pot. "There's still a lot we can do down there. I'll call Jonah's dad to see if he can help. If it's going to be you and your friends, you'll obviously have to have some supervision. And Mom's approval."

"Approval for what?"

We turned to see Mom standing in the doorway, her long silk robe cinched around her waist.

"Good morning," Dad said to her. He gave her a kiss on the cheek.

"What's the smell?" she said, wrinkling her nose.

"Mom, we have a plan," I said.

She shuffled to get a mug as the new coffee began to brew. "There are so many pieces moving today," she said to Dad. "I need to make a list."

"Mom, did you hear me?" I said. "We have a plan!"

She looked to both of us, then asked Dad, "What's going on?"

"Mickey thought all night about this, Chloe. And she has a solution—a good one. Hear her out."

With a nod of encouragement from Dad, I said, "We can all work together—everyone! I can call my friends to pitch in and Dad even said he'd talk to Mark." I nodded toward the back door to indicate Jonah's dad. "They can supervise and we can work while you do your Be Gorgeous demo. It'll all get done, Mom. We'll make sure."

She didn't look convinced. "Too much is riding on this," she said, pouring a cup of coffee. "I don't want any tricks here at the last minute."

"Mom, it's not a trick. All you have to do is work upstairs and check on us now and then," I said, knowing she'd appreciate that last part.

"I think this is a good idea, Chloe," Dad said. "We're all here to help."

Mom seemed to think about it. Finally, she looked at me and said, "Okay, Mickey. Let's see what you can do."

I decided to start with the one girl in town who was still desperately seeking her fame—Kristen.

After her groggy hello, I quickly explained the Hello, Gorgeous! emergency. "You don't have to do this," I said. "But I wanted to let you know what we're doing today. If you want to help, it would be awesome and I'd totally appreciate it."

"Have you talked to Eve yet?" Kristen asked, yawning.

"I've left messages."

"I just need to state for the record one more time—not cool."

"I know," I said, and sighed. "I've been making the rounds of forgiveness since last night."

"You never did tell me why you did it."

"Honestly? I was jealous."

"But you have Kyle!" she said. I almost laughed—*almost*.

"Jealous because I missed hanging out with Eve. Jonah, too. But Jonah and I had a really good talk. I'm still working on Eve, though."

"Well, I forgive you," she said, "if you promise that's the last of the crazy stuff you'll do."

"I promise, one hundred percent," I said.

"Now," she said. "What's happening today?"

"Well, the thing is," I said, "you'll have to miss your appointment."

"My appointment with fame? I mean, Violet?"

"You can say no," I said. "And I'll understand. But I need everyone's help."

"Oh. Well," she said, thinking. "So I won't be in the salon for Be Gorgeous at all?"

"No, you'll be in the basement with us. But," I said, thinking, "I bet there'll be cameras down there."

"That's true." She was quiet for a moment before she said, "I'll do it."

"Really? You mean it?"

"If these renovations fail, then the whole salon might fail," she said. The word *fail* made my stomach ache. "And if the salon fails, no hair or nail appointments for me, ever. I'll turn into a plain, styleless pile of blah.

That can't happen."

"True," I said. "And thanks a million, Kristen."

"You're welcome," she said. "Wait, can I invite someone to help?"

"Of course," I said. "Does his name start with Tobias and end with Matthew?"

I swear I could hear her grin through the phone. "You got it."

Next, I called Lizbeth, who was an easy sell. "I'll do it," she said, before I'd even finished explaining the plan.

"Don't you want to hear my apology first?" I asked.

"Um, okay, sure," she said.

So I told her everything I'd told Kristen, and Lizbeth forgave me, too. All I could think was, *Wow, I had these great friends all along and didn't even appreciate them.*

We all met at the diner on Camden Way where Suse, the old waitress, was friendly with Dad. She let us use the big tables in the back for our meeting.

Mark—Jonah's dad—was there, greeting the friends he and Dad had called. "Get some food, if you want," Dad said, passing a menu to them. "It's on me. Going to be a long day."

I spotted Kyle through the doorway into the main dining area looking for us. I raised my hand, and when he spotted me he smiled and came back.

"Hey," I said. I'd only texted him the plan, so I was surprised that he was the first of my friends to show. "Thanks for coming."

"No problem," he said, putting his hands in his pockets.

"You can sit down," I said. "My dad said you can order anything you want. It's on him."

"What about me? I plan on ordering the whole menu."

Jonah stood next to his friend—I'd completely missed seeing him walk in right behind Kyle.

"Hi, Jonah," I said. "Thanks for coming."

Soon, Lizbeth and Kristen arrived with Tobias and Matthew. I'd warned everyone that this was going to be a messy job and to dress in clothes they could really get dirty, but I guess all Kristen heard was a chance to dress in a special outfit. She wore overalls rolled up thick at the ankle and her hair pulled back in a red handkerchief. I wasn't sure if she was dressed up for the cameras or Tobias, but either way she looked supercute. Matthew was dressed pretty much the way he usually dresses—collared polo and jeans—but it was probably his weekend polo because the colors were faded and there was a tiny tear on the white collar.

"Mickey," Dad said, coming to my side. "We better get going if we're going to pull this off. You're in charge here."

I nodded, taking a deep breath as I told myself I could do this. *We* could do this. Together. It was just after seven, and we had a lot to do in a short amount of time.

"Hello," I said to the group, standing up from my seat. "Hello!" I called louder, hoping to quiet everyone. It didn't work.

"Everybody listen!" Kyle yelled.

That worked.

"Um, thanks," I told him.

"It's going to be great," he said, just to me, giving me a little wink.

Before my heart could race out of control, I turned to the group, who were now all looking at me expectantly.

"Thank you all for coming. It means a lot to my family, and I know Cecilia will be blown away by this. But there's a lot to do, and not a lot of time, so I guess we should get started."

We divided into teams so we were all responsible for one thing—like buying supplies at Home Depot (that took a crew of five), working on lighting (Dad had some electrician friends involved), doing the flooring, and installing all the new equipment that was set to arrive this afternoon. My friends and I were on paint duty. Soon we were organized and ready to go.

"I better go see how my mom is," I told my friends, who were just getting their food. "Thanks so much for helping me out, you guys. It's really cool of you."

"It's going to be fun," Kristen said, setting down her orange juice. "We're like an extreme home makeover crew."

"And you might finally get to be on TV," Lizbeth said, teasing.

"What? Wow, I never even thought of that."

"*Right,*" we all said in unison.

"I'll text you when it's time to come over," I told them. "But you guys will have to come right away. We're on a major schedule so you can't mess around. And make sure you come in the back."

"Yes, Miz Wilson," Jonah said.

"I'll walk you over," Kyle said.

I ignored the goofy smiles coming from the girls.

We started to leave and I was about to say good-bye when they all catcalled, "Wooooo!" Totally and completely embarrassing. Why couldn't anyone grow up?

Once we were outside, Kyle said, "That was annoying."

"Clearly we're the only mature people around."

We crossed the street and headed down the sidewalk. "So, um," Kyle began. "I guess I don't have to text you." I looked at him. "You know, since I'm seeing you now. I asked last night if I could text you?"

"Or we could text instead of talk?"

"Very funny," he said. "But really, last night was cool. Maybe we can do it again sometime," he said.

I think I knew what he was saying but I said, "Totally. I'll talk to the girls." I had so much on my mind today that I couldn't think about my first date with Kyle (my first date ever!) right now.

"That's not really what I—"

"Well, here we are!" I said, stopping in front of Hello, Gorgeous! I didn't want Mom to see me with Kyle in case she started asking questions. "Listen, thanks again for helping. I really appreciate it."

"You don't have to thank me," he said. "It's going to be amazing. That Cecilia chick is going to be blown away when we're all done."

I looked into his eyes, those soft brown beauties with long lashes, and I have to admit I melted a little. I managed to nod my head, mutter *thanks*, and head inside.

The salon was quiet, no energetic stylists gossiping, no hair dryers blowing, no clicking of heels on the marble floors. Just a distant shuffling noise that I knew was coming from Mom in the basement.

Downstairs, she was scooting a large plastic trash bin across the floor in her heels and sleek pants.

"Mom, let me do that," I said, rushing over to her.

"You're going to get dirty."

"We need to make sure this space is cleared before Mark and your father arrive with the paint," she said, eyeing the space. "These boxes need to be moved. We need a trash pile."

"Okay," I said, "but let me do it. You have to look good for your demo."

"The demo is the last thing on my mind," she muttered.

"Let us worry about this. I promise we'll take care of it." I took out my phone and started texting. "I'm getting them over here now to do this."

"The salon doesn't even open for another two hours," she said—still not looking at me, I might add. I wasn't sure if it was on purpose or not.

"I'm just saying," I said, "that they'll be here soon and will help do this."

They all showed up five minutes later, and right away Mom was directing us to move this here, take that out to the alley, get that down from there, sweep this here . . . on and on. She definitely had us sweating, but nobody was complaining.

Half an hour before the salon opened, when the stylists—and Cecilia—showed up, Dad texted that he was on his way with the paint supplies.

"Mom, go upstairs and get yourself ready," I said.

She eyed the space from the bottom step, not ready

to head back up yet. "Maybe we should clear this space over here . . ."

"Mom! We got it!" I said. "Shoo!"

Reluctantly, she left. Soon I'd have to go upstairs to do my regular job as salon sweeper. I couldn't ditch work on a Saturday because of my own mess-up, and I couldn't ask all my friends to come help me paint and not do the work myself. I was stuck doing both. I had no idea how I'd pull it off.

CHAPTER 20

"Mickey, could you please get that styling cream I asked for?" Devon asked as she walked her client back from the sinks.

"I'm getting it now," I said, carrying an armful of butterfly clips to Violet.

Handing them to her, she said, "No, I said the large ones. These won't work."

"Oh, sorry!" I said, turning and heading back again.

"Hey, Micks, you going to the back?" Giancarlo asked. "Could you bring me some extra foils?"

"No problem!" I said, walking as quickly as I could without looking like I was frantic, which I totally was.

I passed Mom on my way, and in the second we passed she asked, "Everything okay?"

"Great!" I said, because everything had to be okay,

even though I needed to be in seven places at once. I wasn't even supposed to be up here this long. I'd come upstairs to find a bucket to fill with water so we could wash off the paintbrushes. I'd been sucked into all the needs of a crazy/typical Saturday at Hello, Gorgeous! instead.

In the storeroom, I dumped the small butterfly clips, grabbed some big ones, and tried to cradle them in my arms. With my other hand I picked up a stack of foils. Heading toward the floor, the basement door flew open and Kyle said, "Hey, you got that bucket yet?"

I thought my head was going to explode. That, or I was going to have a nervous breakdown.

"I'm going as fast as I can," I said, my voice a bit wobbly. But I wasn't going to cry. There wasn't enough time.

"Are you okay?" he asked, furrowing his brows at me.

"Fantastic!" I said through a tightly stretched smile.

"Hey, Mickey, calm down," Kyle said, reaching for some of the things I held. "Let me help you with this."

"No!" I said, a bit too harshly. "Sorry, it's just that if Mom or Cecilia sees you, it'll make me look bad. I can do it."

"Let me at least get the bucket," he said, looking

around the break room. "Can you point me in the right direction?"

"Try that bottom shelf back in the corner there. If we don't have another bucket, maybe a plastic pitcher will do?"

"Thanks," he said, and I started back out to the floor. "And Mickey?" I turned to face him. He had a soft, relaxed look on his face and seeing that calmness made me take a deep breath. "It's going to be okay."

I delivered the foils to Giancarlo and the clips to Violet and headed back to the basement to pick up my paintbrush.

"Mickey!"

I turned to see Devon standing with her fist propped on the hip of her black-and-white striped halter dress, tapping the toe of her yellow platform heels.

Oops!

"Getting it!" I said.

After dashing back to get Devon her styling cream, I finally made it downstairs to pick up a roller.

"How's it going?" I asked Kyle as I started rolling paint on the wall like Jonah's dad had shown us.

"Great. It's kind of fun painting," he said, concentrating on the wall. "I told my mom last year I wanted to paint my room and she said no because she didn't want to do it. But it's easy. I could do it on my own for sure."

"So today is like a teaching day, huh?"

"Big lesson day," he said. "We should get some sort of extra credit."

"Mickey!" my dad called from the other end of the basement. He pointed to his watch.

I looked at the time. "Be Gorgeous!" I explained to Kyle as I dropped my paint roller and headed for the stairs.

He laughed. "You too!"

Upstairs, as I closed the basement door behind me, Cecilia appeared, startling me.

"Hi there, Miss Mickey!" she said. The scent of her musky perfume wafted around me. She wore a new rhinestone chain on her cat's-eye glasses that I really liked. "I've only seen you in flashes today. How's it going? Excited about your mom's demo?" A camera wavered behind her, trying to fit me in the frame in the small space we stood in.

"Yes, it should be very fun!" I said. I tried to subtly glance around her to see inside the salon—it was already pretty crowded with people there for the demo.

Cecilia leaned against the wall as if settling in for a long chat.

"I hear she's doing some sort of retro styles?"

"I think so," I said, because I wasn't sure.

"I'm just wondering," Cecilia said, "if it's a bit odd.

Isn't Devon's specialty retro looks?"

I immediately became defensive. "Devon's specialty is rockabilly. Like, rock 'n' roll of the fifties. But not like poodle skirts." Devon wouldn't be caught dead in one of those.

"Yes, I know what rockabilly is," she said. "I'm just wondering if it's strange that your mom is doing retro as well. What era is she doing?"

"I'm not sure," I said. "I doubt the same thing that Devon does." I hoped so, anyway. Mom wouldn't do that—would she?

"Well, it'll be interesting to see," she said. The noise level rose from the floor, and I could see Mom's head bobbing behind Cecilia. She was looking for me.

"Yep! Sure will!" I said, trying to be as calm and friendly as possible. "Well, I better go see—"

"What do you think of the renovations? Everything going smoothly down there?"

"So well!" I said, with even more enthusiasm. I'd seen the show enough times (as in, every single episode) to know that she wanted to get a little dirt out of me about some dramatic downfall that might be taking place. The cameras were down there but she couldn't see anything until the reveal. And I wasn't about to tell her a thing. "Anyway, I better get back to Mom. Lots to do!"

I ducked around her, making a dash for the floor.

"Mickey!" I heard for the tenth time today.

Chairs were being set up and the crowd immediately went to take their seats. I helped Megan move in some more chairs, stacking a few near Giancarlo's station.

"Is that some new look I'm not aware of?" he asked, pointing to my head.

I immediately touched my hair. "What? Is it frizzed out? Is there something in it?"

"Here," he said, taking my shoulders and turning me to his mirror. "A new spray-on paint trend? I'd go for a darker color, though. This blends too closely to your natural color."

"Ugh, very funny," I said, trying to scrape the buttercream paint out of it.

"Here, let me," he said, picking up his brush. He gently removed the paint and made my hair look a bit more fabulous in the process.

"Thanks, GC," I said.

"Everything okay down there?" he asked. "You and your mom seem on edge. Normal for you but not for Chloe."

"Everything is great," I said, looking over at Cecilia. She stood in the doorway, watching every movement of the staff and clients. I wondered if I should warn Mom about what she'd said about doing another retro demo. But Mom was talking with the customers while she finished setting up, and I knew that there wasn't time to change it.

The demo finally got started and yes, Mom did a retro style, but she managed to make it look new and modern. She showed how to do a nineteen-forties, almost Hitchcock do with soft curls and strands pinned back on the sides. The women loved the classic look, and I was surprised at how easy it was to do. Sticking with her elegant theme, she then demonstrated a modern take on the French twist. She left a few tendrils gracefully framing the model's face. It was a who-cares take on the prissy style that looked sophisticated yet young. It was the best Be Gorgeous demo we'd ever done, and I'm not just saying that because she's my mom. Everyone went crazy for it, and I was positive she'd sell a ton of the products she'd used in the demonstration.

I looked to see what Cecilia thought of the whole thing. She was completely unreadable. I saw Mom glance at her a couple of times, probably trying to get a read, too.

"Mom, that was amazing," I said once the crowd had thinned out.

She let out a deep breath and looked back at Cecilia. "Did Cecilia say anything? What did she think?"

"She wondered why you were doing a retro look since that's Devon's thing."

"Really? What'd she say? Did she seem displeased?"

"No!" I said, backtracking when I saw the look on her face. I shouldn't have said anything. "She was just curious, that's all."

"Maybe I should talk to her," Mom said.

"I'm sure it's fine," I said. Why did I tell her that? Clearly my next projects should be not lying, and learning when to tell the whole truth. "Don't worry, Mom," I tried to reassure her. Then I jetted back to the basement.

???

Downstairs everyone was still painting, but they were really close to being done. Well, except Kristen and Lizbeth. Their section was half done, and Lizbeth was painting a heart on Kristen's cheek with a fine brush.

"Where's Dad and Mark?" I asked as a cameraman captured Kristen and Lizbeth painting. Kristen's hair still looked perfect in the red bandana, and she kept her body angled toward the camera as Lizbeth painted her cheek.

"Outside talking to the flooring guys," Kyle said as I dipped a roller brush in paint and got back to work. "How'd it go up there?"

"It was good," I said, rolling the paint on one of the few remaining sections. "I guess. Cecilia said some stuff to me before the demo and I'm kind of worried she didn't like it. If she didn't like it then that's bad. The demo is a major part of Mom's salon and since it was her day to do it . . . she'll be humiliated." *And I'll be humiliated. Even more for getting Mom into this whole thing in the first place.*

"I'm sure she loved it," Kyle said.

"Hopefully."

"Come on, Matthew," Lizbeth was saying. "Just a little bit!"

"No way!" he said, backing away from the paintbrush she held toward his face.

"Just a tiny little heart. Or whatever you want!" she reasoned.

As Matthew tried to back away from her he spotted another brush on the floor. He quickly bent to dip it in an open paint jar and held it out to Lizbeth. "Come any closer and you're getting it!"

"Just a little, tiny something on your cheek. It'll look so—"

"Don't even," he said.

"You guys," I said. "Come on. We have to finish this."

They totally ignored me. Besides, Tobias couldn't be outdone, no matter what it was. He took the roller brush Kristen had just put down and went toward both girls.

"Don't you dare!" Kristen laughed, backing away. She tried to hide behind Lizbeth, but Lizbeth managed to keep Kristen in front of her.

"Seriously," I said. "You guys."

Lizbeth kept backing herself and Kristen away from Tobias's outstretched hand. "Lizbeth, watch behind you," I warned.

Tobias lunged for the girls, and they screamed and jumped back, knocking over a can of paint. I watched in slow motion as it spilled over the drop cloth, oozing toward the baseboards. They didn't even notice.

"Stop!" I said. "Lizbeth, knock it off!" She stepped in a puddle of paint, and that's when it really hit the fan.

"What is going on?" a voice boomed from the stairs.

Mom.

We all turned to see her standing, horrified and confused, on the stairs, with Dad and Mark right behind her.

"Mickey!" Dad said, coming down around Mom. "What are you kids doing?"

Everyone froze. I moved my eyes but not my head to look at Lizbeth and Kristen. I'd never seen them look as scared as they did now. Welcome to the wrong end of a Chloe Wilson smackdown.

Mom, Dad, Mark, and another camera came down the stairs. Lizbeth and Kristen stood close together, and I swore I could see them shaking.

"Everybody out," Mom said, not wasting a moment. Neither did my friends. They ran up the stairs like the place was on fire. I started to follow them, but Mom said, "Mickey—stay."

"Come here," Dad said from over by the spill. I walked over. "Help me with this."

We pulled the drop cloth over the paint—luckily no damage was done.

"Mickey," Mom said, stomping toward me and Dad. "I appreciate your friends helping but this is exactly what I was afraid of. We should have never left you unsupervised."

"It's going to be fine," Dad said in a calm voice. "Okay, Chloe? Everything is going to be fine."

"Do you see what time it is?" she asked. "We have less than four hours and this place is still a mess. Do you understand how much more work still needs to be done?"

Suddenly, she stopped. Her eyes looked at one of the two cameras filming her. She stood up straight, popped her chin up, and said, "You're right. It's fine. We'll get it done."

"Don't worry," Dad said, and I'm sure he knew she had a bonus moment of panic with the cameras catching her mid-meltdown. "We're ready to do the flooring. Then the crew can bring in the equipment."

"It's still a lot," Mom said. "Can it be done in time?"

"Yeah, probably," Dad said. Mom looked at him nervously and he said, "I'm sure it'll be done. Nothing to worry about."

"Mom, I'm sorry we made a mess," I said.

She looked at me and said, "I'm sorry for snapping at you and your friends."

"Get yourself back out on the floor," Dad said to Mom. "Let us finish up in here."

Mom nodded. "Let me know if there are any problems, or if you need anything."

After she went back upstairs, I thought for a moment Dad was going to yell at me. But he just grinned and shook his head. After helping him clean up the mess, paint had smeared on my smock.

"What a shame," I said to him. "My poor, beloved smock might be destroyed forever!"

Dad winked and said, "You better get yourself back up there, too."

Before I went, I asked Dad, "You think we're really going to pull this off? Save the renovations and make Mom and her salon look good on TV?"

"Yeah, I'm sure it'll be just fine," Dad said. But he had a far-off look on his face, like he were wondering if it were true.

CHAPTER 21

We were all back at the diner—me, Kyle, Jonah, Kristen, Lizbeth, Tobias, and Matthew. Dad had sent us here as another treat for all the work we'd done—and because we were starving. I didn't realize how hungry I was until a burger deluxe with extra-crispy fries was set in front of me.

"How mad was your dad about the paint?" Jonah asked. I sat between him and Kyle, with the others across from us.

"He wasn't mad," I said. "But he did look worried about getting it all done in time."

"They'll make it," Kyle said, like he was absolutely sure.

We'd done all Dad felt comfortable letting us help with, and he sent us here to wait until it was time for the reveal. We'd either show how much we'd done or show how big we failed.

And by *we* I mean *me*.

"What about your mom?" Kristen said. "Did she totally blow once she kicked us all out of the basement?"

"She didn't kick you out," I said.

"But she was mad," Lizbeth said. "Not that she didn't have every right to be—Tobias."

"What'd I do?" he asked innocently. Lizbeth shook her head.

"It's just that her salon means everything to her," I said, feeling like I had to defend her. "She has a lot of pressure on her, all because of me. If this show doesn't end well, her salon could totally crash."

"It's not going to crash," Lizbeth said. "And your mom is amazing. We all think she's a rock star."

"I wish I could have worked longer," Tobias said. "I totally could have laid that floor and installed all that equipment."

"Like you know how," Kristen said.

"Dude, I totally know how."

Kristen took in a breath and said, "What'd I tell you about calling me dude?"

"It was fun to do," Matthew said, his collared polo the only article of clothing at the table that was paintless. "Thanks for letting us help, Mickey."

"Please. Thank you for coming," I said. "I can't believe you all came out to help me and my mom. It honestly means a lot to me." I almost said, *Especially after all the messing up I've done*, but I realized that by this point, they understood—otherwise, they wouldn't be here.

"We're here for you, Mickey," Lizbeth said.

"All of us," Kristen added, then swatted Tobias's hand away as he snatched an onion ring from her plate.

"Yeah," I said. "Almost everyone."

I didn't mean to, but just like that I put a cloud over the table. Everyone was quiet for a moment, staring at their food.

"Sorry, guys," I said. "I just wish Eve could have been here. Not because I want an extra helper, but it would have been even more fun. I should never have done what I did." I looked to Jonah, who had his body turned to me but kept his eyes focused on the door beyond. "And I'll never do it again. I promise all of you that I'm going to be a better friend."

"Oh, Mickey," Lizbeth said. "It's going to be okay."

"I know," I said, even though I didn't.

"Maybe you should talk to Eve now," Jonah said.

"I told you," I said. "I tried. She won't listen. Not that I blame her."

"No," Jonah said. "You should talk to her *right* now."

"Jonah, I've left five hundred messages. I can't—"

"Will you look?" He pointed toward the door. I turned and there was Eve, walking uncertainly toward us.

My heart dropped for a moment. Then it started to race. Was she here to yell at me in front of everyone and tell me what a terrible person I was?

She slowly walked toward us. "Hey, guys," she said.

"Hi, Eve," Kristen said, looking between us.

"Want to sit down?" Lizbeth asked.

"Give her your seat." Kristen nudged Tobias.

"Here, sit here," Jonah said before Tobias could move. He stood up and gave Eve his seat right next to me, then took the empty one on the other side of her.

"Thanks," she said, sitting down. Her hair was pulled back in a loose ponytail and her face looked bright and clean. "So how'd it go today?"

"Great," Kristen said. "We're just waiting to see how it ends."

"It's going to be amazing," Lizbeth said. "Who needs professional painters when you have us?"

"Agreed," Tobias said. "I can't believe anyone freaked out about these so-called pro painters not coming. Do you know how many times I've painted the walls in my house? It's not that hard."

"I think we did a pretty good job," Matthew agreed.

I sat watching this, wanting to say something but

not knowing where to begin. Eve and I had been through a lot. I had so much I wanted to say to her, starting with an apology, but I didn't know how, especially with everyone there, looking between us, wondering what was going to happen. Why had she even come?

"We're just finishing up lunch," Lizbeth said. "You want something?"

"No, thanks," she said, her hands in her lap like she didn't know what to do with them.

I picked at my fries, trying to think of something to say short of blurting out *I'm sorry!*

"Hey!" Lizbeth said. "I have a great idea. Why don't we all go to the Waffle Cone for dessert? I could *so* go for some ice cream."

"I don't know," Tobias said. "This place has the best blueberry pie—" He stopped abruptly, Lizbeth having just whacked him in the ribs. "I mean, uh . . . ice cream sounds awesome!"

"Great, let's go, then!" Lizbeth said, and everyone started tossing their napkins on their plates.

"We'll see you in, like, five, okay?" Kyle said as he got up.

"Okay, yeah," I said, swallowing hard as everyone dashed out. Finally, it was just me and Eve. And then, it was very quiet.

"Subtle, isn't she?" Eve said, breaking our silence.

"Yeah," I said. "Very. Listen, Eve."

"Mickey, I have to say something first," she said. I braced myself. "I just want to say that this is bad. I don't know what to do."

"I know," I said, sinking. "Eve, I'm so sorry. I messed up so badly this time. And I know it. I got caught up in you getting caught up in Jonah."

"But why did you care?" she asked. "That's what I can't figure out. If you really liked me as a friend you wouldn't have done this. To me *or* Jonah."

"I know!" I said. "You're right. I told Jonah this already but I just got jealous. That's all there is to it. I'm ashamed of what I did but I didn't know how to react seeing my two friends go off and leave me."

"We didn't leave you."

"I know you didn't, but for a while it felt like that. I just wanted to hang out with you again. I was being selfish," I said. "I didn't do it to be mean or hurt you. I definitely didn't do it to almost break you two up."

She rested her head on her hand. "I was so upset yesterday when you made me think that Jonah had bailed on me. You knew he hadn't, and you knew I thought he had. That's so unbelievably not cool, Mickey."

"I *know*," I said. I felt like I was drowning. I had no excuses. I had nothing left to say.

"Look," Eve said, sitting up straight and folding

her hands in front of her. "I had a hard time leaving my friends in Ridgeley when we moved here. Especially my best friend, Marla. I feel like you and I became friends really fast. And that's cool, don't get me wrong," she said, turning briefly to face me. "It's just that a lot has happened since I moved here, stuff between us, and maybe we should kind of back off for a little while."

Tears began to well in my eyes as I heard the words. *Back off?* "What do you mean?" I asked, because it sounded a lot like breaking up with a friend.

"It's just," she began, then looked at me with this sad smile. "I'm not saying I don't want to be friends. But maybe we don't have to do everything together. It took me and Marla like six months to become best friends. And I'm sure you and Jonah didn't become best friends the day you met."

I wanted to tell her that we had, but I didn't. I was too stunned to speak. My chin quivered.

"All I'm saying is that I think we should take it easy for a little while. I still want to be friends, but maybe we don't have to try so hard. And honestly, I do feel like you have to earn back my trust. Too much has happened. I know Jonah forgave you for this, but to me it's a really big deal."

"It's a big deal to him," I said. "To me, too."

"I don't want to fight. I just want you to know

that . . . I need some time. Okay?"

I nodded. "Okay." I wiped my eyes on my napkin, feeling worse than I ever had. My big mouth had lost me a best friend.

"So, can I still see the salon?" she asked. "I'm dying to know what changes were made."

"Of course you can come," I said. "If you want to."

"Of course I do," she said. "The salon is where it all started for me in Rockford."

We walked down the street to meet our friends, who were wolfing down the best ice cream in the Northeast. Today, though, even the smell of freshly baked waffle cones and the promise of finally tasting that new tiramisu flavor couldn't cheer me up. When I thought of how the story of the salon might end, I felt like taking the first train out of town. Because the only thing that could make the day worse would be for Cecilia to hate the changes—and for my own mother to hate me for setting it up. No pressure there at all.

CHAPTER 22

My phone beeped, indicating a new text had come in. It was from my dad. I gasped.

"It's time!" I said.

"Let's go!" Kristen said.

We scrambled across the road to Hello, Gorgeous! Inside, we spotted some changes right away. The spot where Karen's manicure station had been was now a full makeup station, and I knew they'd put it there to use the natural light that shone through the front windows. Megan's station had been expanded, too, and now had a new counter where we'd sell high-end brushes and combs. It also gave more space for clients in the waiting area. Rowan's former room was now a storage room and the break room was that and only that.

"Megan!" I said. She stood at reception like she was standing at attention. "It looks great!"

"Let's hope Cecilia likes the rest of it," Megan said.

Looking out at the stylists, I saw that they were eager to hear the verdict, too. They'd closed the salon after Mom's demo to finish the rest of the renovations. But some of our best clients had come back for this moment. Since just about everyone in town knew what was going on, they all wanted to hear what Cecilia von Tressell had to say.

"Where's Cecilia?" I asked Megan.

"She's down there now," Megan said. "Should be back up soon."

"I think I'm going to be sick," I said, my stomach churning.

"It's going to be great," Lizbeth said, throwing her arm around my shoulders.

"I hope so," I said, leaning into her.

"Will there be food?" Jonah asked.

We all rolled our eyes and shook our heads at Jonah. Except Kyle, who punched him in the arm. "We just ate," he said. "Twice."

"I was just asking," Jonah replied.

Mom walked up with Dad from her office. I could see the tiny worry lines between her brows.

"She's going to love it," Dad said. "Just wait."

"Chloe." We looked to see Violet standing in the back near the door to the basement. "They're ready."

"Thank you, Violet," Mom said. She took a deep breath.

"You look great and the salon looks great," Dad said. "We don't need anyone's approval."

"I'll try not to worry about what she or anyone else thinks," Mom said like a mantra, like if she said it enough times, it would be true.

"That's the way," Dad replied encouragingly. I could tell, though, that Mom only sort of believed her words. She respected Cecilia, and I knew she wanted her approval as well, even if she couldn't admit it.

Cecilia appeared in the doorway leading to the break room and down into the basement. She and Mom started toward each other.

"Hello, Cecilia," Mom said, reaching out to shake her hand. "It was wonderful having you here this week."

"Thank you, Chloe," she said, giving her a firm shake. "It was wonderful being here."

We all watched as they eyed each other, old-West style. Mom tried to look relaxed, but Cecilia's face held a new level of steeliness that I couldn't read.

Cecilia turned to face the group as the cameras moved around to film all of our reactions. "First off," she began, "I'd like to thank you for opening up your salon to us. I know it's been quite disruptive, but I hope it's worth it in the end."

"Thank you," was all Mom managed to say.

"I got to know you, your stylists, and even your daughter," she continued. I blushed. "And I must say, I've never seen a team quite like this before."

My heart beat rapidly. I wondered if Mom would remember to breathe.

"Would you care to show us the changes you've made, Chloe?" Cecilia asked.

"Yes," Mom said. "Of course."

Mom led Cecilia—and her cameras—around the salon and showed her all the first-level changes. But of course, the real change was downstairs.

Mom, Cecilia, and the cameras went down. Dad and the salon staff followed. I wanted to be there for Mom and the salon, but it wasn't my place to go. Then, Dad turned and motioned for me to follow. I lit up and started toward him immediately.

"Your friends, too," he said. "They helped with this." I excitedly motioned for them to come with us.

We tiptoed down as quietly as eight anxious people could. When we got a view of what had been done, we all stopped in stunned silence.

The basement looked incredible, like the 2.0 version of the main floor of the salon. The creamy butter-colored walls we painted gave the room a warm feeling, and the entire back wall had a cream-and-black damask wallpaper that was utterly elegant. A silver-and-crystal chandelier hung from the center, pulling the whole look together, shining a soothing light through the basement.

More than that, though, the basement now had everything it could possibly need to be run as a full-service salon. Two rooms had been built into the back corners—one for massages and the other for waxing. Karen's manicure station had been moved down here and expanded, giving her (and her clients) more space. Now she wouldn't be squeezed between Megan and Devon. The display of nail polishes was even bigger than it had been before. There were two whole rows of the new summer colors, including one called Industrial Age that was gold with silver flecks—just like Kristen had wanted!

We couldn't help but gasp at what we saw.

"You all were involved in what happened downstairs?" Cecilia asked, eyeing each of us. We all nodded in unison. Cameras steadied on Cecilia, Mom, me, and my friends. We waited to hear what she had to say.

"Hello, Gorgeous! was a wonderful salon when I first arrived here a week ago," Cecilia began. "But it was underused and wasn't living up to its potential. So I asked Chloe here to do just that." She turned to look at Mom. "I was fortunate enough to meet the wonderful staff of talented stylists and see how they all worked. And although I was mostly impressed," she said, pausing to look at everyone, "I do believe that there can be some updated training. The techniques I saw here are not bad, but they could use some improving."

My stomach dropped, and I couldn't believe this was happening. I looked to Mom, who had a pleasant expression plastered on her face—which was turning a slight shade of green.

"I'm a firm believer," Cecilia continued, "in ongoing training to stay on top of new techniques and to prevent laziness and bad habits. I'm recommending that Violet, as the salon manager, take courses and then teach them to the rest of the staff. I believe this should be mandatory for all stylists.

"As for the changes in the salon itself, after the initial inspection, I asked Chloe to see where she could improve the space and make her salon even better than it was a week ago. Thankfully, those zombie rats I heard about turned out to be myth."

She looked at me and grinned. I couldn't smile back because I kind of wanted to die.

"Seeing this space down here, I have to say I'm impressed. However—can a spa be luxurious in a basement? This is something I gave a lot of thought to. After seeing this, I wondered still if it was high-end enough. I had to question the quality of work that was done."

I held my breath. "I'm happy to say," Cecilia continued, "that Chloe has done something extraordinary. She's proven Hello, Gorgeous! to be . . . a Best Tressed Salon!"

Cheers erupted throughout the salon. A huge grin spread across Mom's face, the first true expression she'd worn all week. Everyone let loose and clapped and whooped wildly. It was a week's worth of tension released at once. From the top of the stairs, Cecilia's crew presented a cake, balloons, and sparkling cider for everyone to celebrate with.

And then, my favorite part of the show after the reveal—awards. Cecilia handed them out to all the stylists for the work they'd done that week and what they excelled at.

Cecilia presented Violet with the Cool Head award. "Because through all the chaos of a salon, Violet keeps her cool—and has a fabulous head of hair." Violet graciously accepted her award, and yes, her golden hair looked perfectly trimmed.

Devon received the Goddess of Retro Rock award. Giancarlo received the Most Original Style award— "For the ability to uniquely style hair and the clothes he himself wears," Cecilia joked.

Rowan got a Tiny Quarters award for working in such a small space for so long. "I didn't mind it," she said. "But I won't miss it." Finally, Karen got the All Shades of Awesome award for the beautiful hands she pampers every day.

"Now, for a very special award," Cecilia said. She turned her rhinestoned glasses on me. I about froze to the spot, a camera swooping in on my stunned expression. "Mickey, who we all know is Chloe's daughter, was the one who texted her mom's salon in to the show and got us here to Rockford. Mickey, I know you've worked here for your mom after school, sweeping the floors and being an overall help to the stylists. They've all told me how much they appreciate your help, and what an amazing young stylist you are in your own right. And so, we'd like to present you with the Future Superstylist award."

The whole salon started clapping, just for me. My friends patted me on the back, and Mom beamed from across the salon. I couldn't believe it was all happening. Not only was Mom's salon a success on the show, but Cecilia von Tressell herself recognized me as someone who could one day be like her.

"Now, we don't have a traditional plaque for you," Cecilia said. "I hope instead you'll accept this." From a bag she pulled out a piece of clothing. "Your mom and I agreed that plastic is just not the right feel for a salon of this caliber. We hope you'll like wearing this instead."

It was an adorable dark pink apron with ruffles around the edges and the Hello, Gorgeous! logo across the pocket.

"Thank you!" I said, taking it and immediately tying it around my waist. "I love it!"

"Now, for one last thing," Cecilia said. "I've truly never done this before, but I've never been more impressed by a salon, or its owner. So I think it's a great time to help shake up my show a little bit, and help you take Hello, Gorgeous! to the next level."

My mind raced at what else Cecilia could possibly do for us. It was starting to feel a little too good to be true.

"First off, the Be Gorgeous demo is such a wonderful idea. We went crazy for it, and love the idea of bringing expert knowledge to the client. We thought of how we could make it better, and for the longest time we came up with nothing—it was simply perfect. But then we realized it did have a major flaw." I held my breath. "The problem," Cecilia said, "is that not enough people have access to it. So we thought—why not put it online? Create a new section of your website, record the demos each week, and you'll have an entire archive of styling tips."

That was why Cecilia was a great businesswoman!

Cecilia said she'd be providing Mom with a camera and video-editing software to get the team started.

"Finally, I have one more surprise," Cecilia said. She turned to Mom and said, "Chloe, you show such leadership here and take such good care with all your stylists. It's clear you treat them like family. It's also clear that you're an incredible stylist, with so much knowledge to teach others. And so, if you'd agree, we'd love to have you as the lead Head Honcho on our next *Cecilia's Best Tressed* show."

The salon let out another whoop of excitement, clapping and cheering for Mom. I hollered right along with them. This would mean even more good publicity for the salon! After a week of emotional ups and downs, Mom finally started to crack. She got the tiniest bit teary-eyed, and held back those tears as desperately as she could. When Dad stepped beside her and hugged her shoulders, she rested her face in his chest for a moment before coming up for air.

"I'd absolutely love to," she finally said.

We all started cheering again. We'd done it. All of us, together.

Finally it was time to cut the cake, uncork the apple cider, and really celebrate the week we'd had. Everyone dug into cake (post ice cream!) and had a cup of cider.

Just as the celebration got started, Eve said to Jonah, "I better get going."

"You're leaving?" I asked, my heart sinking. I wanted her to celebrate with us. "You have to have some cake."

"It's okay," she said. "I should really get home."

I knew that if I hadn't lied to her Friday night then she would have been here the whole time, through it all.

"Everything looks great, though, Mickey," she said. "I'll have to beg my mom for a spa appointment."

"I'll get one for you!" I said. Even I could hear the desperation in my voice. Like I could buy back her friendship? I guess I still had a lot to learn.

"I'll walk you out," Jonah said to her. "Here." He shoved his plate of cake into my hands. "Save this for me."

My and Eve's friendship may have changed, but my friendship with Jonah was back on track. I was happy for that, at least.

He walked Eve out, leaving me alone with Kyle. Next to us, Kristen attempted to feed Tobias cake and Lizbeth and Matthew argued over what was better— tennis or golf.

"So, can I ask," Kyle said. "How'd it go with Eve at the diner?"

I shrugged. "Not so great. She's still talking to me, but barely. She said I have to earn back her trust. What about you and Jonah?"

"Pretty upset, but he said if I played it cool he could forgive me." He cut into his cake with a plastic fork but didn't take a bite. "You know, he's the reason Eve showed up at the diner. Jonah called her while you were upstairs."

"Really?"

"Yeah. She didn't want to come but he convinced her to talk to you." He poked at his sugary slice of cake. "He's a really good friend. To both of us."

I stared down at Jonah's cake in my hands, realizing just how true it was. "I know. The best."

Before I knew what was happening, I was accosted on either side by Mom and Dad, hugging me so tight I smashed some of Jonah's cake on my shirt.

"I can't breathe!" I called. I knew Kyle—and the cameras—were watching, but I didn't care. I was happy with the way things were turning out, even if they weren't perfect.

"Well," Mom began, letting me loose. "I have to say that up until a half hour ago, I had no idea how this whole thing would go. And, Mickey, I just want you to know that I'm more proud of you today than I ever have been. You never doubted the salon or me for a second, and that helped keep me sane this whole week."

I almost told her that I'd been a wreck all week and if I had fooled her into thinking I was calm it was because she'd fooled me into thinking she had it all under control. But I didn't. Instead, I told her I loved her and gave her another big hug.

Cecilia and her cameras did final interviews with the staff. I even saw her talking with Kristen to get a client's perspective. Across the room, as my friends ate cake and the stylists sipped cider and congratulated one another on their awards, my eye caught Kyle's. For a moment, I was sure he'd been staring at me. We'd had awkward moments and easy moments. How come sometimes I could hang with him as easily as I could with Jonah, but other times—like now—he made me so nervous that I almost (*almost*) couldn't eat my cake?

One thing I knew for sure—I had to end that awkwardness, once and for all.

CHAPTER 23

I thought Saturdays at the salon were busy. After word hit town on Sunday that the salon had been deemed a major success by the biggest hair celeb around, Sunday was busier than ever.

Rowan and Karen were totally slammed with facials, waxings, manicures, and pedicures. Mom immediately drafted up some job descriptions for the new employees she'd have to hire. If people who called couldn't get one of the new services, they went ahead and booked with one of the stylists, just so they could be in the salon Cecilia von Tressell had deemed Best Tressed.

I was running around like I always do at the salon, but now that we were officially two levels, I had to run that much more. And because there was that much more space, there were that many more clients—including Ms. Carlisle, my English teacher.

She was just about to go into the little room for a

massage when she spotted me.

"Hello, Mickey," she said, the cotton robe cinched around her waist. Her face was makeup-free and her hair was slicked back into a ponytail. She looked relaxed even before she went in for the massage. "I was wondering if I'd see you here."

"Hi, Ms. Carlisle," I said. It always felt awkward to see a teacher outside of school.

"You know, I wanted to tell you," she began, tilting her head as if to see me in a different way. "I haven't finished grading all the tests from yesterday yet, but I did read your essay on friendship. I thought it was clever how you used a real-life example of unconditional friendship when you spoke of your friend Eve. Well done."

Thank goodness! I didn't know how I did on the rest of the test, but at least I did one thing right. "Thanks, Ms. Carlisle!"

She smiled. "See you in class, Mickey."

After that I felt an extra spring in my step as I raced around the salon. When I brought Cynthia, Karen's assistant, some extra cotton I noticed Lizbeth sitting in one of the new pedicure chairs, testing the back-massage settings. Her mom was heading into one of the small rooms for a massage.

"Hey, there," I said. "What do you think of all this?"

"It's so amazing," she said, looking around the

basement—now anointed The Underground. "I feel like I have to talk quieter down here. It's so relaxing."

"I know," I said. "I have to slow down when I come down the stairs."

Lizbeth leaned back in the chair, finding the perfect massage setting, while Cynthia dipped her feet in the warm, soapy water below. "Kristen and I were talking," Lizbeth said, "and we think now that this crazy week is over, we should have a real girls' night."

"Agreed," I said. "But really—no boys allowed."

"Hey, I can do it if you can," she said with a smile.

"Please! You can't keep away from Matthew for two seconds."

"I don't see him anywhere here," Lizbeth said, looking around. "But I do know that you and Kyle hung out alone Friday night. With food. That's a date."

"First of all," I said, "we had both been exiled. Food under extreme circumstances doesn't count."

"It's a date," Lizbeth said, grinning at me as the balls of the massage chair rolled up her back. "That means you've been on two now."

"We have not," I said, now fully blushing.

"Friday night plus Thursday after school—you, Kyle, and Bended Brook. Total date."

"That was *not* a date. I was only covering for Jonah, who flaked out on him. I was doing Kyle a favor."

"Right," Eve said. "And who paid for dinner

on Friday?"

"I don't want to talk about it," I said, because she was starting to convince me.

"But come on, Mickey. Be honest," Lizbeth said. "You like him, don't you? It's okay to admit it."

"I know," I said. I guess I did like him. I liked him and I didn't have to act crazy about it. I liked him and I still worked at the salon and hung out with my friends (when they were around, that is) and I didn't act like someone else when I was with him. Okay, maybe I was a bit goofier around him, but I couldn't help it. Maybe that's just what happens when you like someone. You want them to like you back so you think about every move you make and everything you say, hoping they don't think you're full of dork.

"Fine, I admit it," I said. "I like him. *Like* him, like him."

"You know, Mickey," Lizbeth said as Cynthia worked her feet and the chair worked her back, "being a girlfriend isn't so horrible. And it definitely doesn't mean being someone you're not. At least, it shouldn't."

"I know."

"So if you like Kyle, and he obviously likes you, then you should see where that might go. Ask him out."

I got a little sick feeling in my stomach. "On a date?"

"Why not?" She smiled. "You've already been on two."

I thought about how I felt when his hand was in mine and how easy it was to talk to him, even when it was just the two of us.

"Maybe," I said. "I don't know."

"Call him now," Lizbeth urged.

"No way," I said.

"Mickey, do it," Lizbeth said.

"I don't think I get reception down here," I said. I pulled my phone out of my new apron pocket and looked at the screen. I had four full bars. "He's probably not even around. I doubt he'll answer."

"Come on," she nudged me. "Call!"

What did I have to lose? I could just do it now and get it over with. So I opened my contacts and, heart pounding, searched for his name. What if I'd misread him this whole time? What if he didn't think I was cool? Or pretty? What if he thought of me as just a decent chick to hang out with when Jonah wasn't around? What if he told me—

"Mickey!" Devon called from the stairs. "You have a visitor."

I looked at Lizbeth. She turned to Devon and asked, "Is it a boy?"

Devon nodded. "Kyle, he said."

"Oh my gosh," Lizbeth said, practically squealing. "Meant to be!"

I started toward the stairs with Lizbeth calling,

"Text me!" as I left. I turned and waved before I lost sight of her.

Upstairs, Kyle stood next to a five-foot potted plant by the door as if he wanted to hide behind it.

"Hey," I said.

When he saw me, a smile spread across his face and he didn't look uncomfortable anymore. "Hi, Mickey." He grabbed his skateboard, which had been leaning against the wall. "I'm not going to get you in trouble, am I? Coming by?"

"I don't think so," I said. "Everyone is pretty slammed."

The salon was buzzing, but Giancarlo had enough time to stop by Megan's desk and give me and Kyle a once-over.

"Want to go outside?" I asked, eager to escape those kinds of looks.

We stepped out on the sidewalk, a cool breeze blowing down Camden Way.

"I didn't come by for any reason," he said as we walked slowly. We stopped between the stationary store and the flower shop next to it and I leaned against the brick wall. Kyle dropped his board, then propped a foot on it, sliding it back and forth. "I was around and just thought I'd say hi, see how the new space is going."

"It's great," I said. "We're busier than ever."

"Nothing's exploded or burned down yet?" he said.

I smiled. "You sound like Jonah." I felt jittery around Kyle, but in a good way. Excited, like something amazing was about to happen. "It's funny. I was just about to call you when you came in."

He looked genuinely surprised. "Really?"

My throat became dry, but I wanted to push through. "Yeah, I was wondering. If, um, after work tonight—I mean, when I get off work, like around six. I was wondering if you wanted to do something. Go somewhere or hang out. We never did get to go to the Waffle Cone. Together, I mean."

It seemed like there was about forty-five minutes of silence before he answered, "Yeah, sure. That'd be awesome. Should I come back by the salon?"

"If you don't mind?"

"No problem," he said. "I'll come back at six."

"See you then," I said. He popped his board and caught it in his hand. He smiled, then dropped it back down, hopped on, and skated down Camden Way. For a moment I watched him go.

When I went back inside the salon, Giancarlo was still there in the front, almost as if he were waiting for me.

"Mickey," he said, tapping the toe of his neon-green boat shoe. "Tell me that boy is finally your boyfriend."

Was he? After two sort-of dates, his willingness to

help out at the salon, and his helping me through my problems with Eve, could I pretend anymore that he wasn't?

I smiled, thinking about Kyle's thick curls and that crooked front tooth. I thought of how he liked me exactly as I was.

Did I now have my first-ever boyfriend?

"Yeah," I said with a smile. "I think he is."

Enter the Get *Gorgeous* Contest!

The grand-prize winner will get gorgeous with a fabulous collection of Lip Smacker® products, a haircut at her local salon, and a complete set of four *Hello, Gorgeous!* books signed by the author! (ARV: $138.00)

Five runners-up will receive a copy of the newest book in the *Hello, Gorgeous!* series, *#4 Swept Up*, signed by the author. (ARV: $6.99)

See official rules on the next page.

✁ -

Get *Gorgeous* Contest!

Enter for an opportunity to win a fabulous collection of Lip Smacker® products, a haircut at your local salon, and a complete set of four *Hello, Gorgeous!* books signed by the author! Just answer this question in 100 words or less: **What makes someone gorgeous, inside and out?**

Send your answer, along with this entry form (or a photocopy of it), to:
Penguin Young Readers Group Marketing, Attn: Get Gorgeous Contest,
345 Hudson Street, New York, NY 10014.
All entries must be postmarked by November 8, 2011, and received by November 15, 2011.

Full Name: _____

Age: _____

Mailing Address: _____

Parent or Legal Guardian's Name: _____

Parent or Legal Guardian's Telephone Number: _____

Official Rules for the Get Gorgeous Contest
NO PURCHASE NECESSARY. A PURCHASE WILL NOT ENHANCE YOUR OPPORTUNITY TO WIN.
Open to residents of the fifty United States and the District of Columbia, ages 7 to 13.

HOW TO ENTER 1. To enter the Get Gorgeous Contest (the "Contest"), read these Official Rules and submit your answer to the question, "What makes someone gorgeous, inside and out?" Your entry must be on an 8 ½" x 11" sheet of paper, using both sides if necessary, and limited to no more than 100 words. Entries may be typed or handwritten. All submissions must be included with an entry form, which can be found in the back of Hello, Gorgeous!: #3 Tangled by Taylor Morris (the "Author") or downloaded from the Author's website at www.taylormorris.com. Each entry form must include your first and last name, full mailing address, age, and name and phone number of parent or legal guardian. Entries must be sent by US mail only to Penguin Young Readers Group Marketing, <u>Attn:</u> Get Gorgeous Contest, 345 Hudson Street, New York, NY 10014. Limit one entry per person. **2.** To be eligible, all entries must be postmarked on or before November 8, 2011, and received on or by November 15, 2011. Submissions by fax, email, disk or any other electronic means will not be considered. **3.** Entries will not be returned. By entering the Contest, contestants agree to abide by these rules, and represent and warrant that the entries are their own and original creations, and do not violate or infringe the rights, including, without limitation, copyrights, trademark rights or rights of publicity/privacy, of any third party. **4.** Entries are void if they are in whole or in part illegible, incomplete, or damaged. Grosset & Dunlap, an imprint of Penguin Young Readers Group ("Sponsor") assumes no responsibility for late, lost, damaged, incomplete, illegible, postage due or misdirected mail entries. Sponsor and its parent, subsidiary or affiliated companies are not responsible for technical malfunctions of any kind which may limit the ability to participate, or by any human error which may occur in the processing of the entries. If for any reason the Contest is not capable of being conducted as described in these rules, Sponsor shall have the right to cancel, terminate, modify or suspend the Contest.

JUDGING 1. On or about November 28, 2011, six (6) winners will be selected by a qualified panel of judges chosen by Sponsor. **2.** Entries will be judged based upon clarity, creativity, and relevance to the topic, with equal weight being given to each criterion. The decisions of the judges and Sponsor with respect to the selection of the winners and in regard to all matters relating to this Contest shall be final and binding. **3.** Winners will be notified via telephone or mail.

PRIZES 1. One grand-prize winner will receive a set of four Hello, Gorgeous! books (#1–4) signed by the Author (Approximate Retail Value ("ARV") = $28.00), a Lip Smackers® party pack (ARV = $10.00), and a haircut at a local salon of winner's choosing (ARV = $100.00). Haircut prize will include the cost of the haircut up to $100 and will be pre-paid by Sponsor. Winner will be responsible for scheduling an appointment and notifying Sponsor of time, location, and contact number. All additional expenses associated with the haircut portion of the prize including but not limited to taxes, fees, gratuities, additional coloring or styling services exceeding the $100 limit and transportation to and from the salon are the responsibility of the winner unless otherwise set forth in the Official Rules. Five (5) runner-up winners will each receive a copy of Hello, Gorgeous!: #4 Swept Up (Book #4) signed by the Author (ARV = $6.99). **2.** In the event that there is an insufficient number of qualified entries or if the judges determine in their absolute discretion that no or too few entries meet the quality standards established to award the prizes, Sponsor reserves the right not to award the prizes.

ELIGIBILITY Open to residents of the fifty United States and the District of Columbia ages 7 to 13. Employees of Sponsor and its parent company, subsidiaries, affiliates or other parties in any way involved in the development, production or distribution of this Contest, as well as the immediate family (spouse, parents, siblings, children) and household members of each such employee are not eligible to participate in this Contest. Void where prohibited by law. All state and local restrictions apply.

GENERAL 1. No cash substitution, transfer or assignment of prizes allowed. In the event of the unavailability of a prize or prizes, Sponsor may substitute a prize or prizes of equal or greater value. **2.** All expenses, including taxes (if any), related to receipt and use of prizes are the sole responsibility of the winners. **3.** Winners may be required to execute an Affidavit of Eligibility and Release. The affidavit must be returned within fourteen (14) days of notification or winner will forfeit their prize and another winner will be selected. If a selected winner is under eighteen (18) years of age, his/her parent or legal guardian will be required to sign the Affidavit. Should the ARV equal or exceed $600.00, winners shall be required to provide a Social Security Number or an Individual Taxpayer Identification Number to Sponsor for issuance of a 1099 Form. **4.** By accepting a prize, the winners grant to Sponsor and the Author the right to edit, publish, copy, display, and otherwise use their entries in connection with this contest, and to further use their names, likenesses, and biographical information in advertising and promotional materials, including on the Author's personal website without further compensation or permission, except where prohibited by law. **5.** By participating in the Contest and/or accepting the prize, contestants release Sponsor, its parent, subsidiary, and affiliated companies, authors whose books are promoted hereby or the agencies of any of them, from any liability, injury, damages, cost or expense, including reasonable attorney's fees, arising out of or connected to participation in this contest or the acceptance, possession, use or misuse of any prizes. **6.** Any dispute arising from this Contest will be determined according to the laws of the State of New York, without reference to its conflict of law principles, and the entrants' consent to the personal jurisdiction of the state and federal courts located in New York County and agree that such courts have exclusive jurisdiction over all such disputes.

WINNERS LIST For a copy of the winners list, send a self-addressed, stamped envelope by May 22, 2012, to Penguin Young Readers Group Marketing, <u>Attn:</u> Get Gorgeous Contest, 345 Hudson Street, New York, NY 10014.

SPONSOR Grosset & Dunlap
An Imprint of Penguin Young Readers Group
345 Hudson Street
New York, New York 10014